ıl

elov

leph

1

LADY WITH A COOL EYE

Things at the Plas Mawr Adventure Centre in North Wales have been going well, but cracks have now begun to appear in the cheerful facade of the school. Charles Martin, the warden, is a weak man with an unfaithful wife, Bett, who has driven him to drink. Jim Lithgow and Nell Harvey are both instructors and appear to be having an affair—and Lithgow is married; Bett, it seems, is also having an affair with another married instructor, Rowland Hughes; and supervision of the boys when they are out in the hills seems most inadequate. And then Bett is found dead in her husband's crashed Jaguar, which she could barely drive, submerged at the foot of the cliffs some miles away. Further developments show that what is at first assumed to be accident or suicide, is in fact a murder case. Miss Pink, one of the school's directors, puts two and two together and realises that the school is being used as a cover for something more serious than a few love affairs . . .

LADY WITH A COOL EYE

Gwen Moffat

·BLACK·
DAGGER
·CRIME·

First published 1973
by
Victor Gollancz Ltd

This edition 2005 by BBC Audiobooks Ltd
published by arrangement with
the author

ISBN 1 4056 8517 4

British Library Cataloguing in Publication Data available

Printed and bound in Great Britain by
Antony Rowe Ltd., Chippenham, Wiltshire

Chapter One

I T W A S A cold clear morning with a sprinkling of snow on the tops. In the hanging valley below the ridge Miss Pink was startled to realise that the depression which she had thought empty was full of figures approaching purposefully through the boulders.

'Quite sinister,' she commented. 'You could take them for guerillas in a war film.'

'It's the silence,' Ted Roberts pointed out. 'They've been trained not to chat when they're going uphill. Nell doesn't have much time for superfluities.'

'*We* always talked nineteen to the dozen when we were young,' Sir Thomas recalled nostalgically.

'The present generation takes its pleasures seriously.' The fourth director of Plas Mawr Adventure Centre was the youngest, but John Beresford had grown daughters and, on the question of youth, held himself superior to his childless colleagues. Roberts and Miss Pink, lawyer and magistrate respectively, who had been observing youngsters (and adults) pass through the courts for decades, glanced his way politely, then back at their main party. They were close now: ten boys, gasping a bit despite the distant appearance of ease, and led by an expressionless young man with a broken nose whose bulky clothing didn't hide the fact that his wide frame carried no spare flesh. His eyes flickered over the directors, he grunted what might be taken for a greeting but he didn't stop.

'A man of few words—Slade,' Beresford observed quietly. The boys plodded past, the more confident grinning self-consciously at the group beside the track. A girl brought up the rear, long-legged and slim in breeches, gaiters and very good boots. Her

5

pale hair was caught back in a ribbon. She stopped in front of the directors and regarded them levelly.

'They all move like guides,' Miss Pink said in admiration.

'It's the pace,' Nell Harvey told her, 'we start slowly and work up a rhythm.'

'When I started,' Sir Thomas said (he was over seventy), 'people tore ahead, then stopped, and every time you caught them up, they moved off again.'

'You have to adjust to the capacity of the weakest member of the party,' Nell said. He blinked.

'Very civilised,' Beresford commented, 'but that restricts the range of the group as a whole. Do the others find it irksome?'

She stared at him. 'Possibly,' she said and moved off. It was obvious she had never thought about it.

'The old guides had a sense of humour,' Miss Pink said with nostalgia as they started to follow.

'It's a different world now,' Beresford reminded her, 'the young have a sense of responsibility instead.'

She made no rejoinder but concentrated on the walk—which anyone but a rock climber would have termed a climb.

Some two thousand feet below them was the valley floor with hedges and Welsh Black cattle on the river flats, stone walls and sheep higher up. Patches of hardwoods wore muted autumn tints for although it was November there had been few frosts so far. Plas Mawr stood in one such wood, distinguished by its exotic conifers, the house a pile of grey stone, the more fanciful Victorian exuberances merged in the mass.

The path that the party was following zig-zagged up the inside of a great horseshoe to emerge towards one end of the cirque. To their south was the sea and Cardigan Bay. To the north stood Yr Aran, the shapely peak that was the climax of the horse-shoe. A smaller mountain, rocky and steep in its last five hundred feet, rose above them.

The first boy staggered as he met the wind. Ahead of him Joe Slade plodded into the dry gale steady as a rock. Miss Pink felt the preliminary gusts and knew a thrill of excitement to be on the tops again.

The others stopped on the ridge for the rear to catch up. Nell, who was the senior instructor, stood relaxed and alert, waiting. Not a brilliant girl, Miss Pink thought, not even striking but healthy, strong and competent. Through the bustle of people and the buffeting wind the older woman felt that she, too, was being watched and, shifting her gaze from Nell, saw that she was observed by Slade. Why should he watch her so intently? Possessive? The two instructors climbed together when they were off-duty. Was there a more intimate relationship? She hoped not and then found herself wondering why. On the surface they were compatible; they both had the same cool expressionless regard, they were reputed to be a good team on hard rock, they had the same interests.... She concluded wryly that she was equating emotional relationships with emotional entanglements—and that marriage meant babies. Facts must be looked in the face, she told herself. If Nell and Joe were anything more than a climbing team, the Centre stood a chance of losing Nell, but just in case, and as an incentive to stay, perhaps a third cottage should be built in the grounds to cope with three married instructors instead of the two they employed now. She made a mental note to discuss this with Beresford that evening.

Plas Mawr Adventure Centre was run with money put up by the huge industrial complex of Global Minerals Ltd., but the idea of it originated with Ted Roberts who, clever but overworked, had so fired Beresford with enthusiasm one wet weekend, that the latter had returned to London and his publishing business convinced that he had evolved the scheme himself. While he persuaded Global, who were terribly self-conscious about their image in the countryside, to part with the money to finance the project, Ted, mindful of Sir Thomas Parry's straitened circumstances since the bottom fell out of the slate market on which the Parry fortune had been built, saw to it that Global paid an inflated price for the old man's white elephant of a mansion. Sir Thomas then moved to the coast where he was looked after by

7

a distant cousin in a glass and concrete villa called Seaview.

Beresford threw himself into the establishment of the adventure centre, seeing the whole project as his own baby and a fitting finale to his working life and the rather tedious autobiography he was writing. He was, in fact, a good catspaw and a hard worker; once shown a course he could follow it with splendid gusto, a characteristic of which Roberts had been well aware.

Ted Roberts had come up the hard way. His father had been a solicitor but *his* father was a quarryman. Ted had been first a junior, then the senior partner in his father's firm and now, retired, he retained a deep and abiding interest in people, particularly in delinquents.

Miss Pink was the odd man out only on account of her sex. Directors were offered a seat on the Board by virtue of their local standing, their knowledge of and interest in youth work and their experience of outdoor activities, but being a mountain centre and with Beresford as chairman, the bias was towards climbing.

Sir Thomas and Beresford were members of the Alpine Club and Miss Pink and Ted Roberts had been active well into middle age and were still strong walkers. She had lived in North Wales until three years ago when the shortness of the growing season (she was a keen gardener) and arthritis drove her to Cornwall where she made a comfortable income from writing features and short stories for women's magazines under a range of pseudonyms.

The first rock peak on the ridge was called Craig Wen. They came down its north ridge in the same order that they'd held on the ascent, with the directors in the rear and behind Nell Harvey, but the youngsters were now moving fast and the gap widened in front of the rearguard who had to be careful of stiff ankle joints.

Now another gap developed as Nell paused and slowed down, watching something below. Then she moved fast along the line to Slade. The file didn't stop.

Miss Pink, waiting politely for Sir Thomas, observed this bit of byplay idly but now, seeing Slade look away from the ridge, downwards, she too looked, but a near spur of rock obscured all but a patch of plateau on the eastern shoulder of Yr Aran.

She moved forward, saw that Nell was letting the file pass in order to take her place at the end again, then the older woman came round the rock buttress and saw all the high upland ahead and below.

There appeared to be nothing remarkable about it; she wondered if there were much difference between a young person's eyes and her own. She continued thoughtfully, hearing Sir Thomas clattering, stiffly but game, behind her. Her glance swept the country. On her right, outside the horseshoe, was the brown bowl of a cwm with a saucer containing black mud and a puddle in the middle: the top basin of a pumped storage scheme. There were disused mine tips in the cwm: triangles of grey scree in the dead grass, and a white road climbed round a spur towards them, to end just below the summit ridge. Here there was a handful of buildings and a wide tarred space where several cars were parked. It was the entrance to an old mine.

'Seen something?' asked Beresford behind her.

'What? Oh, no—nothing.' She still searched the view for some explanation for the instructors' interest.

'What are they up to?' asked Ted, staring.

'Who?'

'The cars at the mine.'

'They'll be walking—the occupants,' Miss Pink said absently, 'you drive to there and you've gained a prodigious height.'

'You leave the car outside the gate.'

'What?'

'It's Saturday too. The men don't work at weekends and the gate's locked. I mean, normally.'

They all stared at the mine entrance while below them, the party of youngsters stopped. Nell looked back and waited.

'Who could—who has a right to go there?' Sir Thomas asked.

'Lawson's Explosives.' Beresford sounded testy. 'But then we should have been informed.'

9

'Why?' Miss Pink asked, 'it has nothing to do with us, nothing at all.' Her tone was acid. ·

She had taken a large pair of field glasses from her rucksack and trained them on the mine entrance.

'Good Lord!' she exclaimed.

'What?'

She lowered the glasses, then smiled ruefully.

'Quite a shock. There's a man with field glasses down there watching *us*!'

'He could be a bird watcher,' Sir Thomas said doubtfully.

'May I?' Ted held out his hand for the glasses and focused them.

'No distinguishing marks on the cars,' he said, 'except—yes— one of them's a police car. Another is a Rover, and there's a Bentley. Apparently a high-powered party, but no one about except the fellow with the glasses. And now he's going into one of the buildings; the door was open. The rest are either in the hut or the mine. Of course we can't see the entrance because it faces away from us. But who are they—apart from the police?'

'There's that Lawson director, what's his name? With a Bentley,' Beresford said.

'Lonsdale,' Miss Pink told him. 'His chauffeur wears uniform; this man's in plain clothes. In any case,' she added with asperity, 'why should a Lawson *director* come up?'

'Well, *you* know,' Beresford said pointedly.

'Even if there were something wrong in the store, they'd never send a director, he's too valuable. They'd send an explosives expert,' Miss Pink said coldly, 'but something's wrong, obviously.'

'It's always been your *bête noire*, hasn't it?' Beresford prompted.

'Of course,' she agreed with more composure, 'I know explosives must be stored somewhere and the more remote the area the better, but you will always put some people at risk and in this case it's Bontddu village, not to mention all the farms and hamlets and our own Centre.'

'They've assured us again and again that the stuff can't explode on its own,' Sir Thomas said.

10

Miss Pink looked at him bleakly. 'I'll never believe it—and I'm of the opinion that that party down below bears me out.'

'Well, let's go down and see,' Beresford suggested.

'As chairman it's your decision,' Ted said, 'but I'd prefer to do it a little more diplomatically. Through the right channels. We can do some telephoning when we get down. If you approach that driver person below he may not say anything and he certainly won't let you in the mine to find his employer, whoever that is.'

Sir Thomas agreed. 'Ring up Global from the house,' he urged.

Beresford raised his eyebrows at Miss Pink.

'We can't do any good here,' she said, 'and perhaps some harm. It might dry up communication altogether. Let's ring London as soon as we get in.'

They moved on towards the main party which continued as soon as Nell saw them coming. Miss Pink wondered what interpretation the instructors put on the weekend visitors to the mine. On the level ridge she caught up, and asked Nell what she thought.

'We were wondering,' the girl said, 'it's probably inspectors.'

'You know about the mines being used for storage then?'

Nell gave the ghost of a smile. 'Why, of course. Doesn't everyone?'

Keeping to a prearranged plan the directors left the others on the pass before Yr Aran and, while the youngsters continued their traverse of the horseshoe, the veterans descended to Plas Mawr and their Board meeting.

It was scarcely surprising that at lunchtime on a Saturday none of Global's directors could be contacted by telephone, at least, none who knew of any troublesome developments in North Wales, the basis for such inquiries being that Lawson's Explosives Ltd., the company which stored massive quantities of stock in old mine levels under Craig Wen, was a subsidiary of Global. Beresford came to the dining room late for lunch and looking frustrated. Ted Roberts, more canny, offered to contact the editor of the local paper but he was playing golf and the best

Ted could do was to leave a message for him to ring the Centre when he was free.

They assembled in the library at Plas Mawr. The warden appeared. It was the first time they had seen him today, and for Miss Pink, who had arrived late last night and gone straight to the Goat Hotel in the village, the first time this visit. She thought the man looked unwell and indeed Beresford had said the warden was feeling seedy that morning which was why he hadn't accompanied the directors on the walk.

Charles Martin had come to the Centre from the Army. He was a handsome, haggard man going soft in the wrong places.

'Are you feeling better?' Beresford asked solicitously as they moved towards the big table.

'Quite, thank you.' The warden met his chairman's eye. 'A touch of colitis.'

Miss Pink thought it was more likely to be liver. There had been no time for the directors to have a drink before lunch but there was an unmistakable smell of whisky about the gathering.

They took their places at the table, produced reading spectacles and the minutes of the last meeting, and the afternoon's business began.

The agenda looked harmless enough but the items provoked discussion which verged on the acrimonious for no obvious reason. When the plans were produced for the two new cottages in the grounds, the objections of Sir Thomas were predictable and there was much discussion on siting, screening, design.

'We've had three designs submitted,' Beresford said, smiling, as if they had all been submitted together rather than separately with Sir Thomas objecting to each. After twenty minutes of circular argument Miss Pink asked:

'Basically why do we need to build? Are the married couples objecting to living off the premises? I would have thought they'd prefer their present accommodation.'

There was a sudden silence, the more marked for the rambling but continuous argument that had preceded it. Sir Thomas was startled, Ted Roberts thoughtful; Charles Martin looked, if anything, sullen. The chairman stared at his papers and aligned their margins meticulously.

'It's sometimes better to have instructors living in,' he hazarded.

'No,' Miss Pink said firmly, 'when they're off-duty, they're off. In any case, both Hughes and Lithgow have telephones and transport and live only a mile or so from Plas Mawr. They can be here in a matter of minutes if necessary, and there is always a duty instructor in the building.'

'One can keep an eye on them better,' Sir Thomas said with an absent-minded air, 'but I still think—'

Miss Pink frowned and opened her mouth to speak but Roberts said: 'Lithgow has no transport so he couldn't be here in five minutes.'

'He takes the Land Rover home,' the warden said.

'That has a bearing on the point at issue,' the chairman remarked, 'unless a man has transport, it's not convenient for him to live off the premises. And Lithgow's cottage in particular isn't satisfactory for the job. The water supply is unpredictable, the hot water system isn't efficient. Staff must have hot baths available when they come home soaked to the skin.'

'I like that better as a reason for building new cottages than the fact that you want to keep an eye on them. That smacks of paternalism,' Miss Pink said. Sir Thomas looked puzzled. She stared at Beresford who refused to meet her eye: 'But then why not improve the existing houses?'

'Because,' Sir Thomas waded in, on firm ground, 'you can go on for ever trying to improve those old places. It wouldn't be economic. They'd never be dry unless you dug out damp courses with a pneumatic drill, and Lithgow's place actually stands on a stream. . . .'

Miss Pink allowed herself to be overborne and they passed the final plans.

'Canoe expeditions,' Beresford read from the agenda with palpable relief, 'the Coastguard have pointed out that we may be going too far along the coast. Porth Bach is a goodish way from the estuary for novices, you know. They say, rightly in my opinion, that with an ebb tide, we could be in a sticky position if anything happened to the safety boat.'

Not for the first time they were reminded that they had no seaman on the Board, but Roberts and Beresford agreed to consult local experts and, since the season was over anyway, the problem of canoes' range was shelved thankfully until a future meeting.

They passed to the next item which was the delegation of authority in the possible absence of the chairman. Sir Thomas proposed that Miss Pink and Ted Roberts should be deputies. This was passed while Miss Pink wondered if the chairman had any specific contingency in mind when he put the old man up to it. At this point Roberts was called from the library to take a telephone call and returned some considerable time later, obviously disturbed.

'A complete shambles,' he exploded, taking his seat again. They waited expectantly, the warden watching him with a curious expression that could almost have been defiance. There was tension round the table; even Beresford's well-bred charm was gone and in its place was the cold mask which is the Englishman's defence against surprise.

Ted was looking through his bi-focals at the agenda, murmuring: 'Local telephone exchanges are a disgrace to the principality!' He met the chairman's eye blandly: 'Where have we got to?'

Smoothly Beresford continued with staff salaries but Miss Pink's attention strayed to the warden. She wondered if the uneasy atmosphere which had prevailed throughout this meeting originated with Martin who had taken virtually no part in the proceedings unless appealed to directly. On these occasions he seemed to come back from a great distance and the effort was embarrassingly obvious. Now, after his momentary interest in Ted Roberts, he had withdrawn again.

Beresford was winding up: 'Well, that's that,' a glance at his watch: 'And now I believe they've put on a delicious tea for us.' He glanced at Martin pointedly who responded with difficulty: 'Oh, yes. Yes. In the dining room.'

He walked to the door, opened it and passed through ahead of the directors. Sir Thomas stared after him in astonishment. Roberts crossed the room, closed the door and came back to them.

'The electricity people,' he said clearly and with obvious restraint, 'have discovered that they've built a pumped storage scheme under a mountain that, for two decades, has been used to store explosives. The party at the mine is the Central Electricity Generating Board, the police, and the highest ranking people from Lawson's who could be found on a Saturday afternoon.'

'But they knew all the time,' Miss Pink protested.

'The suggestion is that they didn't.'

'That's preposterous!'

'We know that. The Press knows it. That's not the point. Either the explosives must go or the reservoirs have to be drained and abandoned and that means the end of their pumped storage scheme. The implication being that Bontddu is at risk since it's below the dams.'

'Then they've always been at risk,' Miss Pink began angrily but Beresford was saying quietly: 'Would that be the real reason for draining the lakes, Ted? The C.E.G.B. knew the explosives were in the mountain when they built the dams. The stuff can't suddenly become dangerous—or can it?'

'No,' Ted said, 'they're talking of evacuating the stuff but they want it kept quiet. Partly I suppose because of the shindig there'll be at what might have happened, and, more practically, because they're afraid of the lorries being hi-jacked when the stuff's evacuated. We're too near Ireland.'

They thought about this for a moment, then Sir Thomas asked how dangerous the evacuation would be.

'Some of it may not be in the best of condition. They've had an explosives expert up but,' Ted's voice cracked with indignation, 'would you believe it, the master plan of the store can't be found and the storemen and the manager have all gone to a football match in Wrexham where, incidentally, the police have failed to find them, and you know what those old levels are like. The

15

mountain's honeycombed with them, and half of them have fallen in. . . . We'd look fine if there were an emergency, a fire for instance. We could all be blown to kingdom come before the sirens went.'

'How did they get in the mine?' Sir Thomas asked.

'They had the keys but nothing more. They must have been wandering around the inside of the mountain like so many blind moles. Perhaps they are still.'

'Knocking gelignite off shelves,' Beresford commented wryly, 'and all the time we were prancing over their heads. How did Howell know all this?'

Ted was surprised at his ignorance. 'The grapevine, of course. A country editor has an information network like the criminal underground. He had a man up at the mine and inside the gate shortly after the top brass arrived but he was forcibly ejected by "an ape with a Cockney accent". Then Howell went up himself (he wasn't playing golf at all) and blackmailed them for the story. He knew it was important with his reporter being man-handled. They told him but he's not going to print anything about the possibility of hi-jacking. That's to be kept quiet.'

There was a murmur of agreement, then Beresford said: 'I can see why you didn't speak in front of Martin.' He collected their eyes. 'I'll contact Global this evening to get the official line on these developments. Meanwhile I think we can take it that we're not going to be blown sky-high within the next half-hour, so I suggest we have some tea to be going along with.'

Miss Pink preceded her colleagues to the door thinking grimly that his brusqueness was dictated by cowardice. As he'd remarked on the mountain: the explosives had always been her *bête noire* but, curiously, now that some of her fears had been confirmed, she was no longer angry. The eye of the storm, she thought.

Chapter Two

THE WARDEN'S WIFE had dull red hair dressed elaborately in what was once called a beehive. Her skin was thick and creamy and from the other side of the room the eyes appeared as black pits in a mask. She was thin and her hipbones showed through an acid yellow dress that was slightly longer than the fashion. Despite the fact that she was only thirty she looked dated and rather worn. Her eyes met those of Miss Pink but there was no reaction, no hint of greeting.

'Hitting the bottle,' Ted observed as he handed his colleague a cup of tea.

'Obvious.' Miss Pink turned to face the window and the rain which was now falling against the sombre shrubbery. 'She looks tubercular,' she added absently.

'I meant Martin. He's gone straight to his flat, I presume. He should be here.'

'I know. There's more wrong than meets the eye. Everywhere.'

'It's not as bad as that surely? This is what comes of having a lady writer on the Board.'

'A sense of atmosphere isn't a monopoly of ladies.' She looked at him straight. '*You* don't feel that there's something wrong?'

He raised his eyebrows. 'I'm the incurable optimist, probably the result of living all my life in a dying community.'

'I would have thought you'd be a pessimist.'

'No. If you do survive, nothing can be as bad as what you've come through.'

'If you look at it that way, I suppose that, beside poverty and decades of unemployment, the problems of an adventure centre are somewhat trivial.'

'They can be put right more easily.'

'Miss Pink,' said a hard bright voice at her elbow, 'do have a cake.'

She gave her attention to Linda Lithgow: a small intense girl whose dark mane almost obscured huge round spectacles.

'Mr Roberts has his priorities right.' She glared at Miss Pink angrily.

'I'm sure he has. You think our problems are trivial too?'

'I don't suppose it's diplomatic to say it, but—' she fixed them with that intent stare, 'are we important?'

Miss Pink had had a heavy day and now she found herself wilting. To be attacked suddenly and without warning by the chief instructor's wife was the last straw. Over Linda's head she appealed mutely to Ted—and saw Beresford had approached.

'Do you mean us as people, my dear, or as an institution?' He was at his most avuncular.

'I don't mean anyone personally, just all of us. Do you think teaching children to climb mountains should be a primary function of life?'

'You think the *Thoughts of Chairman Mao* should be a set work rather than *Mountaincraft*?'

She looked at him in contempt. 'It's not political, it's social. What evidence have we that climbing makes them better people? We don't even have a follow-through.'

'Children need adventure,' Miss Pink said stolidly.

'They need a goal!'

'Could it be the same thing?' Ted asked.

'There's no end-product,' the girl insisted, 'their energies should be channelled productively, like V.S.O. or the Peace Corps.'

'Do you think you should direct children into that kind of work?' Miss Pink asked, vaguely interested despite her fatigue for she knew that the girl was sincere. In Miss Pink's parlance, once the rough corners had been smoothed off, Linda would become a useful person.

'That depends on who does the directing,' Linda said.

'She is saved only by her utter *gaucherie*,' Beresford remarked as she moved on with her plate of cakes.

'She's rather wearing,' Miss Pink admitted, 'Lithgow is well-suited to her. He must be as impervious as a crocodile—armour-plated.'

'One would never feel sorry for Lithgow, even married to Linda,' Ted chuckled.

A large woman in her thirties entered the dining room carrying a large brown teapot. She placed it on a table and, looking round, saw the three directors and came across.

'I haven't had a moment,' she said, smiling, 'they're coming off the hill sopping wet; there's a crop of blisters—it's those new French boots, John—and one sprained ankle: Nell had them make a rope stretcher for practice and they carried him the last mile. They're stoking the furnaces like firemen to keep the bath water hot. Won't it be lovely when we're oil-fired? Will you have more tea?'

Spontaneously there rose to Miss Pink's lips the question: 'Are you running this outfit?' but she said mildly and with only a little emphasis: 'A secretary never stops.'

Sally Hughes glanced at her. 'Linda's helping,' she pointed out, 'and now that all the instructors have finished they're supervising things. Rowland and Jim just looked in for a moment.' They followed her glance to where her husband and the chief instructor formed a group with Sir Thomas and Bett Martin. The warden's wife was animated now and slightly flushed. The group had a curious air of cohesion despite the disparity of its parts.

Jim Lithgow was a small spare man with a grizzled beard and receding hair. Sir Thomas was expounding some point but Lithgow, although immobile in a listening attitude, gave the impression of a coiled spring, his eyes moving over the room like those of an alert bird of prey except that he looked less fierce than mocking. There was no respect in that look.

Hughes, large and a little too heavy, a red-faced man in early middle age, slightly stooped, listened to Sir Thomas with an air of profundity, stroking his chin. Bett Martin stood close to him, her eyes on Lithgrow.

Both instructors, clean but still in their breeches and sweaters, exuded vitality and a smell of wet tweed. Perhaps there is not so much wrong, Miss Pink thought; it's just the one couple. The last instructor came in then: Paul Wright, his hair still wet from the shower, his eyes widening in genuine pleasure as he crossed the room to Miss Pink. She smiled too for she was quite fond of Paul, but she was startled to see, as she looked past his shoulder, answering his greeting, that Bett Martin's eyes had followed him. Ignoring her own group, she stared with unmistakable hostility at Paul's back.

'Soaked to the skin,' he told the directors cheerfully, 'all white and wrinkled like a frog's paw.'

He displayed his small hand which did indeed look chilled and flaccid.

'Where were you?' Miss Pink asked.

'On the crag in the grounds. And for the last half-hour standing immobile on the absolute tip at the mercy of the elements and trying to coax my second up the top crack. I feel as if I've been on the receiving end of a fire hose.'

He looked young and lithe and happy.

'Did you do that thing in the Lake District?' Beresford asked, 'what was it, Hawker something?'

'No Hawkers. It was frantic. I came off the top pitch, and the last two pegs came out—my God! I can hear them now, tinkling against each other—they slowed me down though and I came to rest past the next one. It stopped me being frightened of the thing. I got up it all right after I'd had a breather.'

'Good gracious,' Miss Pink exclaimed, 'you came off the top of *that* cliff! I've never seen anything so forbidding.'

'You know it?'

'No, indeed. I've looked at it. I know where your No Hawkers is. Why the name?'

'Swifts. The first time I attempted the route they were all over the place, hawking flies. The top pitch is a terribly delicate slab, and you know the exposure—I swear they were tipping me, those swifts. I felt like a weak sheep with ravens trying to knock me off. We retreated that time but the swifts had named the climb for us.'

'What fun you have,' she said sincerely.

'We're in something of a fix,' Beresford said, placing two sherries carefully on the table and seating himself. They were in the residents' lounge of Miss Pink's hotel which was in the village of Bethel and about a mile from the Centre. The chairman had finally contacted Global and been told to sit tight and keep quiet; everything was under control. On returning to the lounge after making the call, the snub showed in his manner and in his sudden interest in trouble inside the Centre. Miss Pink played up to him.

'There were undercurrents at the meeting,' she agreed, 'you should have warned me. A fix? Is Charles Martin an alcoholic?'

'I wouldn't be surprised, but he's not my main concern—at least. . . . I don't know.'

She looked at him in surprise.

'It's not like you to be so vague, and ever since I had your letter suggesting this evening on our own, I assumed—in fact you implied—that there was something specific to discuss. You mean, it's something other than his drinking?'

He picked up his glass and studied the pale liquid. He pouted boyishly and she knew he was embarrassed but nerving himself, anticipating her reaction.

'I don't like the ideas going round the school,' he said with a hint of defiance, 'all these protest movements. Everyone's mixed up in some group or other. I found a tract about battery poultry houses on the driver's seat of my car this evening!'

Miss Pink allowed herself a smile.

'John! You've put your finger on it when you say everyone's mixed up in something. What do you expect of responsible youngsters—anyone for that matter? It's not a bad thing, you know.'

'Yes, I know what you mean: sewage and—er—so on. That's all very well; it's the potential I worry about. We're in a very delicate position. Nowadays one has to know what one's

21

employees are up to—or at least to know where their sympathies are. You do realise, don't you, that with all this concern about the environment, these kids will be thinking of Global as the enemy? Particularly with this new development: storing explosives not over-far from centres of population. After all, we wouldn't stand much chance if the lot went up, let alone the surrounding villages.'

'They're too level-headed to fly off the handle with such a flimsy excuse. No,' she added quickly, seeing his surprise, 'I don't mean the explosives aren't serious but that the staff will realise that the Centre doesn't bear responsibility for Global's mistakes.'

'The trend now is that we're all responsible for all mistakes. Conversely, that the little man pays for the shareholder's profits. No, it may appear paternalistic but I'm prudent and I want to see those cottages finished and all our staff on the premises where we know what they're up to.'

'There's no further argument; we passed the plans. But I wish you didn't distrust the staff, John.'

'Not to say *distrust* exactly.'

'What's wrong with the instructors?'

'Well for one: Lithgow's too independent.'

'You're a conformist. The Centre's for adventure; any "character moulding" is incidental. You're thinking in terms of Outward Bound and a military tradition. We need men with initiative, particularly the chief instructor. It doesn't matter so much with the others; they should be good at taking orders and, I believe are, judging by their work (you can't fake things in the field and in front of experts) but the chief man, no. He runs the Centre so far as training goes, and I'd rather have a man who was too independent than one who played safe.'

Beresford listened morosely. He hated Miss Pink putting the finger on his conformity.

'A chief instructor's job, in a Centre like this, is full-time: twenty-four hours a day,' he said.

'It shouldn't be; he'll work better for having a life of his own in his off-duty hours.'

'It's a dedicated job,' Beresford persisted, 'Lithgow isn't dedicated.'

'He's competent and he gets on well with his staff and the students. I can't imagine anyone disliking Jim. He's so lively. He could be abrasive if you wanted to be lazy or quiet, but a mountain centre doesn't go in for that kind of atmosphere.'

'You can't pin him down,' Beresford tried again, 'he's as slippery as an eel.'

'Not dishonest.'

'No, I didn't mean that. His attention slips. He's never with you when he's talking.'

'But he's a good chief instructor,' she reiterated, 'that's the crux, isn't it? I believe your dislike is personal.'

'Do you? You may be right.' He shifted ground again. 'But we'd do well to get Hughes inside.'

'*Inside?* Ah, I see. Yes, Hughes is a different kettle—but harmless. Certainly not dedicated, but not independent either. But we can't afford to lose him, because we need Sally.'

'I wasn't talking about losing anyone. Only tightening the bonds. Sally Hughes would be a great asset to any Centre, so long as she stays.'

A small elderly waitress in a frilled cap and apron opened the door.

'Dinner is served, mum,' she said with a little bob, and went out.

'I've seen her before,' Beresford remarked.

Miss Pink smiled. 'Olwen used to be with the Parrys at Plas Mawr. She's a worker—one of the old school. Here, she's chambermaid during the day, waits at night—at least in the off-season. Most informative woman.'

She preceded him to the dining room which was dimly lit, but one lamp made their table a pleasant oasis of light.

'Romantic,' she stated as a matter of fact, then: 'Why should Sally leave?'

'She won't,' he said with certainty, 'Sally Hughes is the kind of woman who, if the children don't come first with her, they

23

come a very close second. They're both doing well at the local school and the girl's taking G.C.E. next year.'

'Is there any question of Hughes wanting to leave?'

'He took me aside this morning after breakfast and made no bones about refusing to continue under Martin.'

'I'm surprised the staff didn't petition you *en masse*; an alcoholic can be ignored if he keeps out of your way but they have an unfortunate tendency to erupt at crucial moments. What did you say to him?'

'I smoothed him down a little and gave him to understand that he would hear more before the weekend was over. He also hinted rather clumsily that he didn't get on with Wright.'

'I did warn you.'

'I apologise. At the time I thought you were way out, as they say. And there are many Centres with homosexuals on the staff, as I happen to know, and these can be some of the best instructors, providing they're not rumbled.'

'Which was your justification for employing Paul Wright. Do you think Hughes has rumbled him?'

'No, he merely dislikes him. Given Hughes' character there would have been violence if he'd guessed the truth.'

Olwen took away the soup plates and served duck. They ate in silence for some time. The Goat was noted for its food, the chef being a formidable lady called Miss Devereux who subsidised her retirement pension by a substantial (and illegal) income from cooking. She had a *cordon bleu*. They didn't touch on the subject of Plas Mawr again until the coffee pot was between them and they were relaxing in the pleasantly intimate atmosphere that follows a good meal. The coffee was strong and black and Miss Pink regarded her Cointreau happily, and gave judgement.

'I think the only person who can damage our interests, I mean the Centre's interests of course, is Martin. In the circumstances, with young people in his charge, there's no doubt about that.'

'He's got much worse recently,' Beresford said, 'he seemed to be holding on for a while, then suddenly he lost his grip.'

'His staff wouldn't suffer fools gladly.' Miss Pink refrained from pointing out that an alcoholic, or even a man who was fond of drink, shouldn't have been appointed in the first place. She felt that this would have been taking unfair advantage of the fact that she hadn't been on the selection committee. But she did remark gently that before the next warden was appointed, the directors might do worse than emulate some American firms and interview, or at least see, the potential warden's wife as well. Beresford agreed and became practical.

'I'll write a letter to Martin. Although with a well-worded hint—' he looked hopefully at Miss Pink, '—he might be induced to resign.'

'That would be kinder.'

'Would you find it very unpleasant?'

'You're going home tonight?' she asked pointedly.

'I must. I promised Janet, and Tim and his wife are coming tonight from Geneva.'

His son was with the World Health Organisation. They talked family for a while then Miss Pink promised to do what she could with the warden the following day and to telephone the result to Beresford in the evening.

'As for the rest of the staff,' she said, 'I don't think the problems are worse than they are with any outdoor activities centres. If anything I would say we're lucky. We have five instructors and two wives. The wives are running the place most efficiently between them and of the instructors: one you say is too independent—but he's full of energy and he's the chief instructor and he needs initiative; another isn't getting on with the warden and one of the juniors. A new warden will solve the one problem and I'm rather inclined to put my trust in Sally to see that any dislike of Paul Wright doesn't develop into open hostility. Sally's clever and knows which side her bread is buttered, whereas Hughes, whatever his capabilities as an instructor (and they're not much; it's his wife we need most) isn't distinguished for intelligence. But Sally can handle him. As for Wright himself: he's an able instructor and has a remarkable way with the more backward children. I don't think we've any cause for worry— once we've found a suitable warden. You can't have any fault to find with Nell Harvey, and as for Slade,' she smiled, 'he's the typical non-commissioned officer, which I believe he was—'

'In the Commandos: a corporal.'

'He's the kind of material that will obey orders without question and see that they're obeyed. On the hill today I felt that they were a good team: he and that girl. I believe they climbed in the Alps together this summer.'

'They did some great routes.'

'I'm not surprised.' She didn't mention the possibility of their marrying and the need for a third cottage. It seemed curiously out of context.

'I hope you're right,' Beresford finished his brandy. 'I *hope* you're right,' he repeated doubtfully, 'but I'd be very grateful, since you're staying on for a time, if you'd keep your eyes open, and if you feel that things aren't running smoothly, you might investigate. And do watch out for any unrest over the explosives situation.'

She sighed. To balance his innate conservatism, he indulged a taste for melodrama—and he was an expert at delegation.

'I'm on holiday,' she repeated.

'You can't help but run into them: on the hill, along the coast. They drink here too; they're probably in the bar now.'

He left soon afterwards to return to his house near Shrewsbury. Miss Pink, on the way to her room, glanced through the open door of the cocktail bar and saw that it was almost empty. The wet night was keeping people in front of their television sets. However, over the shoulder of a burly farmer she saw the auburn curls of Paul Wright. She continued upstairs thoughtfully, not relishing the prospect of tomorrow although there was no doubt about it: the warden would have to go. We shall have trouble with the woman, she thought, if she wants to stay, then she felt a little guilty that she should be concerned only with the fact that the warden drank heavily, and the effects of this, but no one had reflected on the cause.

Chapter Three

S U N D A Y D A W N E D G R E Y and wet. Olwen brought her tea
just before eight and Miss Pink drank it while she listened to the
news on her transistor. The Goat didn't run to radio in the
bedrooms. Israel had shot down a MIG fighter and claimed that
the dead pilot was Russian; another famine was feared in India,
and heavy rain had caused a landslide in Yugoslavia, sweeping a
bus into a gorge where all the occupants were drowned. On the
home front a large cache of explosives had been found near the
Irish border and a bomb had been removed from the ground
floor of a tower block of flats in Belfast before it exploded.

An enquiry into the exposure tragedy on the northern Pennines
had resulted in strong criticism of the warden of the Centre who
had sent the party out in bad weather under the leadership of a
man of twenty.

Miss Pink switched off, knowing that the responsibility didn't
rest there. As in war, it came to roost with the men and women
who had selected the staff originally and then held a watching
brief. Perhaps every Centre should have its staff and routine
periodically reviewed—but that was one of the functions of
Board meetings: held on the premises and, in the case of Plas
Mawr, with the directors accompanying students and staff in the
field. Then how had Martin's deterioration been missed? He
must have pulled himself together for the last Board meeting
three months ago; now he no longer cared. She had thought the
same of his wife yesterday afternoon. The woman's lack of
response had been insolent, nor had she spoken to any of the
directors unless they approached her themselves. It was Sally
Hughes who had substituted as hostess.

She dressed rapidly, reaching a decision. Holiday or no holiday, her first duty was to the Centre. Charles Martin must be

dealt with, but at the same time she ought to try to discover if there were any basis for Beresford's nebulous fears of trouble. The chairman tended to irritate her. Now that she was alone she admitted to herself that there was certainly a curious atmosphere at the Centre, one which she had attributed to insecurity. It was an organisation without a leader. Now she had second thoughts. She remembered Linda's sudden vehemence yesterday afternoon. Was that genuine or had she some motive for hostility other than her arraignment of Plas Mawr's policies?

Towards nine o'clock she telephoned Martin at the Centre. He answered after an interval: a blurred, incoherent voice. He summoned enough energy to agree to come to the Goat at two o'clock and she rang off. Then, in breeches and boots and waterproof anorak, she left the village and started along a muddy track which led eastwards towards the Lithgow cottage. There was a road from the village but Miss Pink was not the kind of woman who walked on tarmac when there was an alternative that was closed to traffic.

As she strode along the sodden hedgerows she reflected that she had been wrong when she had said that Jim Lithgow could reach the Centre in a few minutes if he possessed a car. The cottage was only a mile from Plas Mawr but in that direction the route was an unsurfaced track across fields. With a car he would have to drive to Bethel and then up the valley: more than twice as far.

The cottage was a lonely place, isolated at the side of the mouth of the broad valley and surrounded by trees. These climbed the slopes behind and on either side and were intersected by a steep grass-grown ramp running straight as an arrow to a black hole high in the hill. This was one of the old mine entrances and on each side of the ramp wet spoil heaps gleamed through the thinning leaves.

There were distant shouts and Miss Pink saw that there were climbers on an outcrop of rock above the tree-line. She assumed that they came from an Army encampment which was a field's width to her right, the tops of lorries showing above the hedge.

She stopped in the shelter of a sycamore and took the binoculars from her rucksack.

One climber was on the hard move of a route she remembered with affection from many years ago. She watched with deep interest and approval—and unaccountably suddenly her vision darkened.

Startled, she lowered the glasses to find herself listening to the embarrassed apology of a young man who had approached silently and was now standing in front of her. Never impervious to good manners and a pleasant face she studied him with interest. He was dressed in climbing clothes that were vaguely military in origin. For a while they discussed climbing and she learned that the Army unit came from Cheshire. This man was a lieutenant and, it appeared, an expert climber. When she moved on towards the Lithgows' cottage he accompanied her for a short distance, talking of Alpine routes, then he sketched a salute and took his leave. She noticed that the little finger of his right hand was abnormally short, as if he had lost the top joint, a not uncommon hazard for alpinists who have to run the gauntlet of falling stones. He made his way towards the slope, evidently going to join the climbing party. She looked back after a few moments but he had disappeared.

The Lithgows' cottage was small, one storey high with tiny windows, and overhung by huge sycamores. Linda opened the door. She was wearing a dirty fisherman's jersey and old slacks. She had been crying and she stared at Miss Pink as if the other woman were a stranger. The girl said nothing and in the face of that vacuous stare Miss Pink forgot her fact-finding mission but neither could she turn her back and go away.

'Can I be of any help?' she asked.

Linda sighed deeply and without affectation.

'No,' she said. She sounded utterly exhausted.

'Where's Jim?'

'He said he was going to the Centre.'

'On duty?'

'Preparing the next course. He said.'

'Wouldn't you like a coffee?' Miss Pink asked. The girl studied this innocuous question. 'I suppose so,' she said at last and turned. The movement appeared to start her functioning again and, leaving Miss Pink in the living room, she could be heard filling a kettle in the back kitchen.

The room was dim. There was no electricity. A table stood in the window with a dirty mug, a greasy plate and a bottle of milk. There was no fire. There were dimly discernible climbing photographs on the walls, and two shabby bookcases on either side of the grate were filled with books. Miss Pink recognised the climbing books by their spines and she bent to examine the paperbacks. They were on sociology, psychology, anthropology.

Linda brought two cups of coffee and put them on the table. Without speaking she took the dirty crockery and the milk bottle away. She sat at the table and Miss Pink drew up a chair. It was the only spot in the room that was light.

'This place would depress anyone,' the older woman said with the emphasis on the last word as if she were continuing a conversation.

'Anyone,' Linda repeated tonelessly.

She was, thought Miss Pink, in shock. It was pointless to go to the Centre for Lithgow who must know of her condition if he'd been home last night and had left this morning. Was he responsible?

'I didn't see the instructors at the Goat last night,' she said, 'only Paul.'

The girl looked at her. 'They weren't in the Goat?' she said with a rising inflexion which made it a question.

'Where were they?' Miss Pink asked, feeling her way.

'I don't know.'

She seemed totally divorced from normal social etiquette and . Miss Pink drank her coffee in silence for a few moments while she wondered what was to be done, then she remembered where she could find help.

'I'll send Sally along,' she said and stood up.

'She's got her own troubles,' Linda said tonelessly. She stared out of the window at the rain. Miss Pink sat down again.

'Can *I* help?' she repeated.

'How?'

'I don't know unless you tell me.'

The girl stared at her dully. Miss Pink appeared to relax.

'There's so much of it,' Linda said with a spark of impatience or resentment, 'it's so complicated. Besides, you're his employer really—' She looked at the other woman hopefully.

'It needn't lose him his job,' Miss Pink assured her, hoping that this was true.

'You know? No, you're guessing—but you don't have to be inspired, do you?' Without a change in tone, conversationally, she went on: 'She appears to behave herself in public but her eyes look right through you—insolent. She looks at men the same way: coldly, without expression, like men look at girls' legs when they're drunk. She uses people. She's using Jim. I told him so; I tried to make him *see*. She's foul. She's ruined everyone in that Centre—except Sally—and Paul.'

Her face crumpled and she tore off her glasses.

'Oh God,' she sobbed from behind her hands, 'you must have seen it—all of you. Why did you let it go on?'

'The Board meetings are every three months. I didn't come to the last one. All the same,' Miss Pink said firmly, 'now we know, the situation will be—remedied—'

'They'll all be fired,' Linda said, not without satisfaction, 'and in his position too! I mean, he was in *authority*!'

'Not conduct becoming to a chief instructor,' Miss Pink said but her eyes were kind and she smiled. Whatever had happened, this one appeared to be getting the worst of it.

Linda tried to respond. 'Conduct unbecoming to a gentleman,' she said in a faltering Blimpish voice. She went on more naturally: 'He was a fisherman though, off a Stornoway boat. I met him when I was youth hostelling in the north-west.'

'Where exactly did you meet him?'

'At Lochinver. One night in a hotel bar. So I stayed up there.

I got a job in the hotel. I'd been reading Social Sciences at Birmingham but I lost interest. I was very young then. It was Sutherland was responsible: glorious country, d'you know it?' Miss Pink nodded. 'He loved it too. So when he came back to Lochinver again he signed off the boat and we took a croft north of Kinlochbervie where the road gives out and all the people have left.'

'What did you live on?'

'He had some money. But it cost almost nothing to live. Ten pounds for the cottage for six months and we lived on bread and fish. We burned driftwood and peat.'

'Why did you leave?'

'The money gave out. We quarrelled. It was my fault. I felt I was wasting myself up there. We moved south and he worked in a garage in Fort William for one winter. He loved that and we were happy again although I still wasn't making any contribution to society. He had Ben Nevis at the best time of year (he's a great ice man, did you know?) but when summer came and there was no more ice climbing, he wasn't so keen and he just cleared off. I thought he'd gone for good and I got a job as ward maid in the local hospital but he came back in the end as if nothing had happened. He'd been in the Alps all that time. Then we saw the advert for this place and I thought he might settle down. I wanted a baby, you see.'

'And your studies?'

Linda was returning to normality. She said defiantly: 'They've not been wasted. I'm writing a book—about the clearances in the Highlands, where the landowners drove the crofters out and burned their homes to stop them going back, because sheep brought higher profits than people!' There were tears of anger in her eyes. 'And some of the lairds did nothing. Didn't drive out the crofters but just sat back and watched them die of famine and disease and apathy. We want to go back and start a commune.'

Miss Pink saw that that desire was logical for Linda but she was surprised that Jim should agree.

'Oh, he'll go,' Linda said airily, 'he's game for anything.' She winced.

'Don't persuade him yet. He's a good instructor.'

'Do you really think so?' She was pathetically eager. Miss Pink was finding these emotional oscillations somewhat exhausting.

'If you can hold out a little longer I can promise you things will right themselves.'

'In what way?' She had recovered sufficiently to take advantage of an opening.

'Of course,' Miss Pink said firmly, 'this other business must stop—'

'Oh, it will!' She put on her spectacles and stared through them curiously. 'You mean, you'll stop it?'

'If your own protests haven't been effective.'

'I told him I would go to Mr Roberts on Monday and start divorce proceedings.'

'Mr Roberts is retired.'

'He'd recommend someone.'

'You don't need to do that now.'

'No, that's what he said.'

Miss Pink stood up and prepared to leave. She asked if Linda would care for a walk but the girl said she had lunch to prepare and, apparently eager to show that she was herself again, took a joint out of the oven which she must use as a meat safe, and lit the gas. Miss Pink left the cottage with a jaunty step but as soon as she was out of sight her pace slackened.

She felt drained of energy and emotion but the void was slowly filling with anger and a grim awareness of the job which, she hoped unwittingly, John Beresford had wished on her.

As she trudged slowly back to the village she was only faintly conscious of noise and bustle from the field where the Army was packing to leave. Too wet for them, she thought idly, and was glad the Centre wasn't on the hill today.

At two o'clock she was waiting in the Goat's writing room for Charles Martin. Since this was the off-season there was no receptionist in the hall and Olwen had been asked to send the

33

warden in as soon as he arrived and to see that they were not disturbed.

When, at five minutes past two, Martin hadn't put in an appearance, she told herself that she shouldn't be surprised in the circumstances, but when there was still no sign of him at two-thirty she telephoned his flat. There was no reply.

She waited ten minutes, then rang the Centre which was on a different line. Sally Hughes answered and told her that the warden had gone out about an hour before and not returned. She sounded flustered. In the background Miss Pink could hear women's voices and they appeared to be arguing. Sally said: 'Ssh, *please*!' and a Welsh woman said angrily: 'But I've got to get home, miss!'

Miss Pink asked what was wrong but she had to repeat the question because of the background noise. Sally, choosing her words, said carefully that the kitchen staff had to go home and there was no transport to take them. They lived in Bethel and it was pouring.

'How many women?'

'Three.'

'I'll come up,' Miss Pink said, 'I'll run them home.'

As she drove up the valley she reviewed the transport at the school. If the warden was out he'd be in his own car. That left the Centre's Land Rover, the Hughes' car, Nell Harvey's van....

Unlike the Lithgow cottage Plas Mawr was not dominated by its trees. A vista had been landscaped to the south-west and the sea. The lights were on this overcast afternoon and the sight of boys moving behind the large windows in the library and common room, sitting in window seats reading, was a sign of normal activities, and cheerful.

Three village women were waiting in the hall, their annoyance obvious, their thanks for the lift perfunctory. Rowland Hughes appeared, heavily in charge of the situation.

'This is most good of you, Miss Pink,' he said richly, 'now if you will trust me with your vehicle, I'll run the ladies home.'

Sally came to the door of her office which opened off the hall.

Miss Pink handed her keys to Hughes then she went in the office and shut the door.

Sally explained the situation. The warden had taken the Land Rover, Nell and Slade were both off-duty and had taken Nell's van, the Hughes' car was in the village garage.

'I see,' Miss Pink said, 'and I suppose in his absence Bett couldn't give permission for someone to take the warden's car and to run the women home in that?'

'She isn't in the flat, and the car's not in the garage.'

'But she can't drive!'

'She's passed her test now and drives a little. I didn't know Charles was letting her drive the Jaguar but of course he must be. I mean, if he drove the Land Rover away, she must have taken the car.'

'Quite,' Miss Pink agreed, 'he had an appointment with me at two o'clock,' she added.

'Oh, Miss Pink, I *am* sorry—' she trailed off; even the placid Sally could think of no defence for a warden who failed to keep an appointment with a member of the Board.

'Will you need transport to bring the kitchen staff back for supper?' Miss Pink asked.

'No; supper's cold on Sundays. The boys serve it under the supervision of the duty instructor.'

'And that is?'

'It's me.'

She wondered when she would come to an end of these irritating discrepancies in the Centre's routine. Aloud she asked:

'Who are you standing in for? You're not an instructor.'

'It's the warden's turn today.'

'He asked you to take his place?'

'Not exactly. He went off suddenly after lunch. I happened to be here because I'd come in this morning to type next month's timetable but it wasn't ready so I did something else and lunched here because I hadn't transport to go home, so I happened to be around when the warden left. Someone has to be on duty for the phone and accidents. Forty boys unsupervised in a big building. . . .' She smiled.

'What about your own family?'

'Rowland always lies in on Sunday if he's not on duty, and the children are great readers. I rang Jennifer and told them to come down for lunch but she said they'd manage on their own, and didn't seem pleased that I should imply they couldn't.'

'Where are the other instructors: Paul and Jim?'

'Jim's working on the timetable upstairs, so you see I could always call on him if I needed a hand. Paul's off-duty. I don't know where he is. He wasn't in for lunch.'

Sally went out to make a pot of tea and Miss Pink wondered if she should have a word with Lithgow about his wife but she thought better of it immediately. Her hands were tied by the fact that Linda's distress was occasioned by the relationship between her husband and Bett Martin. It was a charged situation and when she caught up with Martin it was imperative that he should pack his bags and leave right away. If he wouldn't resign, he must be dismissed. The Centre could afford three month's pay in lieu of notice more easily than the couple's presence for that time. With the Martins out of the way the basic cause of trouble would disappear. The Lithgows could be moved into the flat (the Board could work out later what to do about the new warden's quarters) and the couple would get back on an even keel once Linda had recovered from her shock. Despite the depth of this Miss Pink couldn't help feeling that someone was being unduly melodramatic. She was obviously very much in love with her husband and had no cause previously to doubt his loyalty—although there was that long sojourn in the Alps, presumably without letting her know where he was. But climbing and extra-marital affairs were very different things; wives of climbers rather expected to lose their husbands to the one, but not on account of the other, which was why Miss Pink thought that Linda was making too much of it. That gay hard little Scot was no Casanova; in this context he was the pursued rather than the pursuer, she was sure of it, and probably he'd be as glad as his wife to see the back of the Martins.

She crossed to the window to see if there was any sign of a break in the weather. She wasn't depressed by the rain. November was usually a wet month in Wales. Nevertheless there was an atmosphere of *siege* about the school staff and among the wives, and this she deplored. She would have liked to assure them that they would shortly be rid of the trouble, but she ought to see Martin first. No doubt Bett would quickly publicise the fact of their dismissal. However, Sally was a sensible woman who had been carrying all the domestic and administrative duties for too long. It would be kind to give her a hint (after all, she would almost certainly know by tonight) and in view of the incident involving the kitchen staff it might be good policy if the secretary could assure them first thing tomorrow that the school was to have a new principal.

Over tea she said to Sally: 'The warden is very ill.'

They looked at each other silently for a moment then Sally said: 'The staff can't go on much longer like this.'

'They won't have to.'

'Thank you.' Sally was obviously relieved. 'How soon can I tell them—or will you?'

'I must see Martin first; it's rather unethical, telling you before I see him, but the situation is unconventional, to say the least.'

'He's had so much worry,' Sally breathed, almost to herself. She looked up and caught Miss Pink's surprise. 'I won't say anything—even to Rowland,' she added quickly as tyres spurted on gravel outside.

'I'm returning to the Goat now,' the older woman said, 'perhaps you would ask the warden to telephone me as soon as he comes in.'

She found Hughes adjusting the driver's seat in her car. He thanked her for the loan of it.

'Did you see the Land Rover in the village?' she asked. If the warden were waiting for her in the Goat, the vehicle might be visible.

His eyes looked over her shoulder.

'I didn't see it anywhere. Why, did you want to see him?'

She smiled faintly.

'How well did Mrs Martin drive?' she asked.

37

He stared at her in astonishment.

'How the—? How well did—she—drive?'

Fascinated, she watched him recover balance but said nothing herself.

'I've no idea,' he blurted, 'She'd passed her test. I don't know how well she drove. How could I?'

'She's not here, nor is the Jaguar.'

'That's nothing to do with me,' he said loudly, almost shouted —and a steady voice interposed: 'Miss Pink is wondering if she's crashed the Jaguar, I think.'

Sally was smiling at them from the doorway.

'That's what's in your mind, isn't it? And you think the warden's out looking for her.'

'That seems the most likely explanation,' Miss Pink agreed, getting into her car and noting that Hughes walked towards his wife without attempting to hold the driver's door open.

It was dusk: the bad time between daylight and dark, and coming down the narrow road between high hedges, she saw brilliant lights ahead and dipped her own. It occurred to her that this could be the Land Rover and, about to pull into a passing-place, she changed her mind and stopped the car where it blocked the road. Not wishing to take chances on the warden's alcohol level, she left her headlights on, dipped.

The other vehicle approached and the sound of its engine told her it was a Land Rover. It stopped and she walked to the driver's side.

'My wife's gone,' Martin said without greeting or apology, 'she hasn't been home all night—last night. When I got up her bed hadn't been slept in and the car wasn't in the garage.'

'Does she often drive it?'

'She's never taken it before.'

'We're blocking the road,' Miss Pink said, 'turn round and come back to the hotel where we can be comfortable.'

Chapter Four

'I CAN'T BRING the police in yet,' he said stubbornly.

He raised a shaking hand to draw on his cigarette.

They were in the writing room of the Goat.

'How soon would you feel justified in reporting her missing?' Miss Pink asked curiously.

'I don't know. When would you?'

'If my wife had been missing for hours in a powerful car which she hadn't driven before, I would have telephoned police and hospitals first thing this morning.'

'You don't understand.'

She was struck by the similarity between his wretchedness and that of Linda Lithgow. Again she felt a surge of anger against Bett Martin. Such a depth of emotional involvement was unusual in Miss Pink and to make matters worse she was uncomfortably aware that she was finding Martin pitiful. Studying him now she tried to see him and his wife simply as problems which were by no means unique, rather than people responsible for the welfare of children who were, ultimately, in the Board's care. But she couldn't rid herself of the awareness that although his wife's behaviour might be accepted as an excuse for his heavy drinking, he was fundamentally weak and most unsuited for any position of responsibility.

'I asked you to be here at two o'clock,' she told him, 'because it would be better for everyone concerned if you tendered your resignation.'

'I expected that,' he said with an attempt at a wry smile which was spoiled by his trembling mouth.

'You will receive three months' salary in lieu of notice and the Centre will pay the cost of removing your furniture to—your next position. I would like you to go as soon as your wife returns.'

'Suppose she doesn't return?'

'Why do you say that?'

'What makes you think she's coming back?'

'Do you know more about her absence than you've told me? This wouldn't appear to be my business,' she went on, 'but if your wife's absence affects or delays your departure then I'm afraid it becomes the Board's business.'

'All right, all right! I get thrown out because she sleeps around. Am I her keeper?'

'Yes,' Miss Pink said shortly, hiding her surprise, 'I shall not discuss the matter. How you deal with that affair is outside my province but I think the fact that your car is missing should be reported.'

'She can't drive it,' he repeated with a return to his former wretchedness.

'Are you suggesting that someone else took it?'

He thought about this seriously for a moment.

'It would mean them coming in to the garage past the kitchens—and the yard all lit up. . . . Why not? They could skirt round the edge of the light. I don't think I saw her after supper. If she went then, when the women were busy serving in the kitchen, no one would be noticed in the yard.'

'If you think someone other than your wife has taken the car, you'd be within your rights to report it as stolen.'

'If she was with him? You do want to get rid of me, don't you?' he said nastily, and she realised that she was concerned less with his feelings than with the nuisance of his wife having chosen this particular moment to disappear.

'I apologise if I seem unsympathetic,' she said more gently, 'but you must understand that my first consideration is the Centre, although if that were my only concern I'd try to suppress any scandal. Surely you realise that whatever your wife has done, reporting the car missing (and that's publicising her disappearance—or her non-appearance) is going to mean gossip which will involve the Centre, at least to some extent?'

'I'll report it tomorrow; I'll give her a chance. She might come back tonight. Won't you let it rest till morning?'

'I must speak to my colleagues on the Board. Are you going back to the Centre now? I'll telephone you before eleven this evening. Meanwhile, if your wife returns perhaps you will contact me. She may be in a hospital with a bump on her head. Have you thought of that?'

He stood up and said with extraordinary intensity:

'Miss Pink, I apologise if I've been rude but perhaps you'll realise what I've been going through when I tell you that I wouldn't be surprised at any kind of violence that had overtaken my wife.'

About to ignore this and leading the way to the door, she asked sharply: 'Then why were you so anxious to find her this afternoon?'

He appeared genuinely surprised. 'I was looking for my car!'

Over the telephone Ted Roberts said: 'You've told him he's got to resign and he knows he must go tomorrow. You can't do more than you have done. The business of reporting his wife missing is up to him, of course. It seems far more likely in the circumstances that she's gone off with a man than that she went alone and crashed the car. But I think it would put your mind at rest if I made some discreet inquiries. A pale blue Jaguar—that should be simple. I'll ring you back before ten. Meanwhile don't worry. I'll come to the Goat tomorrow after breakfast.'

'Yes,' Beresford said after he had heard her report. 'I was afraid that something like this might happen. Of course he'll have to leave tomorrow (you were quite right to say he'd receive three months' pay in lieu, although paying for his removals . . . well, cheap at the price, I dare say), and so far as the local people are concerned she went first and he followed. In fact, it would be better if she didn't return. You might point that out to him. Discuss it with Ted.'

'How do you propose we suggest to him that his wife doesn't return?' Miss Pink asked. She was starting to feel very tired.

'What's that? Oh, you can't, of course. But I think his present attitude is the right one; I mean, we can all guess what's happened, can't we? It would be in our interests if he doesn't look for her too enthusiastically, not till after tomorrow anyway.'

'You aren't coming back?'

'I was coming to that. I had a call from young Michael: my nephew, you know, he's by way of being a senior director now. Was to have gone to New York on Tuesday: the annual visit, and there's Abigail Hertz to see in New Jersey; she's under contract to us....' Miss Pink shifted her weight as he droned on; she knew what was coming. '... Michael's always been bronchial, and with this tendency towards pleurisy—'

'You're taking his place and going to New York on Tuesday.'

'To London tonight, I'm afraid. Janet's upstairs packing at this moment. But I have complete confidence in you, my dear, you and Ted. I'm empowered to appoint you joint acting deputies since the Board meeting, if you remember. I'll let Thomas know and I'll see that the Minute Book is sent on to you, then you can act officially for the Board if anything untoward comes up while I'm in the States.'

'It appears to have come.'

'What? Now, my dear, I should be there, in an official capacity, I know, but considering the way things have developed since yesterday, there's no one more competent to deal with the situation than yourself. With due respect you have more experience of—er—human frailty than anyone else on the Board—'

'Excepting Ted.'

'Ted? He's been more concerned with criminal cases—but I see your point. A quibble. Then' (triumphantly) 'you make the ideal team. I've complete confidence in you both and I'm sure that goes for Thomas. I may be a competent chairman when it's dealing with matters of organisation and architects' plans,' he chuckled deprecatingly, 'but when it comes to human problems I feel I can happily put three thousand miles between me and the Centre and not lose a moment's sleep. By this time tomorrow everything will be solved. You'll be rid of Charles Martin (you're already rid of his wife), the Lithgows will be in comfortable quarters—and I'll see to it that my secretary gets the advertisement for a new warden out this week. We're paying generously.

One insert in the *Daily Telegraph* should be sufficient. By tomorrow evening you and Ted will be trying to remember what all the fuss was about.'

Miss Pink was alone in the dining room and since Olwen was the only person in the hotel with whom she had more than fleeting contact, there was a certain intimacy between them. They murmured pleasantly over the serving of the meal and Olwen lingered as Miss Pink started to eat.

'Queer thing, that one going off, like,' she observed.

Miss Pink paused over her *sole bonne femme*.

'That one?'

'Her at the Plas: Mrs Martin.'

'Are you related to someone in the kitchen?' Miss Pink asked, not irrelevantly.

'Sassie Owen is my brother's second wife. Assistant cook she is. Emma Jones is cook; I don't have nothing to do with her. My brother's wife has a temper. She thought it very kind of you to send them home in your motor car.'

Miss Pink acknowledged this gracefully, knowing that it was intended as Sassie Owen's apology for the incident that afternoon when the kitchen staff were near mutiny. She finished her sole thoughtfully and said:

'Mrs. Martin couldn't drive very well.'

'She drove well enough.' Olwen had been waiting for her cue.

'She'd never driven her husband's car,' Miss Pink said idly, straightening her place mat.

'Maybe so. She drove it last evening.'

'How far?'

'Now that I can't say,' Olwen's eyes clouded with disappointment, 'but she drove it away from the house. Sassie heard the motor start and that noise—made her look out the window, see. My brother is teaching her to drive and he gets wild when she makes that noise.'

Having sorted out the pronouns Miss Pink deduced that Mr Owen was teaching his wife to drive and that Bett Martin had crashed the gears on her husband's Jaguar.

43

'She drove away?'

'Jumping,' Olwen said succinctly, 'like an old rabbit.'

'I wonder how far she got,' Miss Pink said quietly, 'that's a bad road coming down the valley from Plas Mawr.'

'That one's gone out of the valley. The poliss is related to my husband distantly.' Although widowed for many years, Olwen never referred to her husband as "late".

'You mean the car has left the district,' Miss Pink queried.

'Her too. They all know her.'

'So she drove herself away,' Miss Pink told Ted after he had telephoned and reported that no blue Jaguar had been involved in an accident, neither had Bett Martin nor any unidentified woman been admitted to hospital in the area since six o'clock on Saturday.

'It looks as if she picked someone up,' he said, 'did she take any luggage?'

'I didn't ask Martin. If neither she nor the car is found, you must be right. She's gone off with someone. It's Martin's concern now.'

She told him they were to be acting deputies and he chuckled.

'My visit tomorrow will be official then. We can see the warden off together. Would you like me to telephone him now?'

But she felt that she should carry through the matter which she had started. Telling Ted she would expect him after breakfast, she rang off and dialled the warden's number.

He showed no surprise when he heard that there was no question of the Board's relenting, indeed he seemed surprised that she should have troubled to confirm the earlier decision. However, when she told him that his wife had been seen to drive herself away and that she was alone at the time, there was silence at the other end of the line.

'Are you still there?' she asked, thinking that he seemed more coherent than he had been over the last two days.

'Yes,' he said, 'I was wondering how far she'd got.'

She felt he had a right to know that neither his wife nor his

44

car appeared to be in the area and she told him so, stressing that inquiries had been discreet and unofficial.

'It doesn't matter,' he said heavily, 'so she's left. . . .'

She was about to ask him when he would report the matter but reflected that, as Ted had reminded her, it was now the man's own affair as, of course, was the question whether his wife had taken any luggage. She said goodnight with some embarrassment.

'I'm sorry,' she added sincerely.

'It's all right,' he said and the receiver was replaced too hard, as if it had been dropped.

Chapter Five

It OFTEN HAPPENS after days of rain in the western hills that a dawn will come sparkling fresh with all the wet colours shining in the sun: bronze oaks, pale flames of larches, tawny bracken; and above, the delight of the first snow, with the peaks white against a pale blue sky—which made her think immediately of the missing Jaguar.

It was nine o'clock on Monday morning and she was on the second cup of coffee when Olwen came in quickly to give only a ritual glance at the table before saying: 'He phoned my brother this morning and told him to be there at half past eight to take him to the station: Bangor!'

She stopped, watching Miss Pink who, well aware of the taboo against the word "why", repeated: 'To Bangor!'

'Don't say I told you but my brother's got a big car. A good heart too. Takes people to functions and weddings, to the station if they want. . . .'

An unlicensed taxi driver. Hadn't Olwen mentioned his working in the mines and being on benefit now? Those of the old miners with pneumoconiosis would occasionally supplement their pensions with the odd bit of cash income. She felt honoured by the trust invested in her.

'Your brother drove him to Bangor this morning,' she repeated, necessarily, to keep Olwen going.

'Gone bag and baggage. Left his furniture though. There'll be a message for you at the Plas, shouldn't wonder.'

Ted Roberts came into the dining room and Miss Pink sent Olwen for another pot of coffee. She told him the news.

'I passed Owen about a mile outside the village,' he said, 'but I didn't think to notice his passenger. He's gone to London, has he?'

'What makes you think that?'

'Gone to catch a Holyhead train.'

She smiled ruefully. 'John won't be pleased. I've committed the Board to paying the cost of his removals.'

Sally Hughes fingered the envelope addressed to Miss Pink. She turned it over and studied the flap, poking at it with a finger nail.

'No, don't do that!' her husband exclaimed, 'I *told* you: they're both gone now—cleared off. We're finished with them.'

'But she couldn't drive that car. That's the point, isn't it?'

'Look, there are witnesses: Sassie Owen. After all, why shouldn't she drive it? She'd had enough instruction. The reason you fail your test so many times is a psychological block. Once you get rid of that, you're away. That car's in London now—and she drove it there.'

'You think she'd learn to drive it as she was driving, as it were? Could that happen?'

'Of course it can. Remember that film, what was it called? Where the woman had *never* driven before and she had to drive along a cliff road in the dark and it rains and she doesn't know which knob is the windscreen wipers?'

'That was a film, Rowland. And, anyway, *did* Bett know which knob was the windscreen wipers? It was pouring.'

'Of course she did, She must have done. She left anyway, so what's it matter?' He glared at her belligerently.

'Only that I'd like to be sure she left,' Sally said quietly.

They stared at each other. In the silence they could hear the muffled, institutional noises of the Centre, and the sound of tyres on gravel.

'That'll be the directors,' he said, 'I'm off. Get them to tell you what's in that note.'

He went out quickly. She put the envelope on her desk, sat down, drew a paper towards her and started checking a list.

Miss Pink knocked and came in with Ted Roberts. Sally showed no surprise to hear that they knew the warden had left.

She handed his note to Miss Pink who read it and passed it to Ted.

'He's gone to London and left a forwarding address,' Miss Pink said, 'he asks us to store his furniture until he sends for it. You'd better have the address so that you can forward mail.'

Ted handed Sally the note and she laid it aside.

'Shall I try to find a firm to store his furniture?'

'As soon as possible,' Miss Pink said, 'I'd like to get Linda out of that cottage today.'

Sally looked surprised.

'That place is getting her down,' Miss Pink added. The secretary said that yes, she'd noticed the girl looking rather peaky lately but that she was sensitive and, well, she looked at Ted with a polite smile to include him, things would right themselves now, particularly with Jim and Linda moving in to the building. Ted said that he wanted a word with Lithgow about the safety boat and went out.

Sally smiled more naturally at Miss Pink. 'You can't imagine the relief now they've gone,' she said, 'but we have to restrain our feelings because if we did let go it would imply disloyalty to the Board.'

Miss Pink followed her reasoning with ease.

'Neither Ted nor I was on the selection committee that chose Martin as warden,' she pointed out.

Sally nodded. 'I'd always wondered how he got past you and Ted, although he wasn't nearly so bad when he first came. It became worse as she got more blatant. She was drinking heavily too.'

'Why didn't you tell me?'

'I haven't seen you for six months, and it was obvious that something had to snap. I felt that, given enough rope, she must surely hang herself in the end—' She stopped short and Miss Pink, looking at her quickly, thought she saw her eyes change focus, but it could have been a trick of the light. She went on in exactly the same tone: 'I don't think the Centre suffered; they're grand kids. They held it together. If I say it as shouldn't, you have a very good staff.'

'I know. And if this episode has done nothing else that's positive, it's demonstrated that.'

'What do you intend to do now? I mean, immediately?'

'I'll leave you to find a removal firm. Meanwhile I shall go to see Linda and tell her she can start packing. After that Ted and I would like to sit in on some of the activities for a while: show the flag a bit. You've been carrying too big a load, all of you.'

The fire had been lit when Linda showed her into the dim living room. The table was cleared and the door leading to the back kitchen was shut. Miss Pink felt that she was expected. She guessed that Sally had telephoned ahead. Merely to warn Linda to clean her living room?

She told the girl that the Martins had left and that the Lithgows could move to the flat once the furniture had gone. It had occurred to her as she drove down the valley that Linda might find it uncomfortable at first living in the flat of the woman with whom Jim had been having an affair, so she added: 'If you'd rather not move into the flat, we might try to arrange something else temporarily until the new cottages are built.'

'I don't mind,' Linda said earnestly.

'Good.' Miss Pink hesitated, momentarily at a loss. Linda rushed into the pause.

'I was terribly stupid yesterday,' she began breathlessly, 'for years I've been reading about sexual psychology and all that and when I get involved in an extra-marital affair myself I act like a moron. It was unpardonable and so subjective.' She smiled but her eyes stared anxiously from behind the huge spectacles. 'I'm terribly sorry, and you must have been—you were very kind.'

'Not at all,' murmured Miss Pink, 'but I'm delighted that you can be so objective today. Of course, you have the advantage of knowing it's all over.'

'Oh yes, definitely.' The girl looked out of the window and shifted a cactus on the sill. 'He's going to stay; I mean, if you wanted his resignation he'd give it to you. I don't know about her, of course. But after you said yesterday that he was a good

49

instructor, even when you *knew*—I told him that, when he came home—he promised me it's all over, so you see, it will be all right.'

'Of course it will.' Miss Pink was fighting to hide, not surprise but astonishment. A suspicion crossed her mind. 'Have you any idea where Bett Martin went?' she asked.

'I've no idea at all,' Linda said coldly.

'You're not interested?'

'Why should I be?'

'Let me get this clear. Jim has been seeing too much of a woman. Which one?'

'Why,' Linda appeared taken aback, 'I told you yesterday!'

'You thought you did. So did I. But you never mentioned a name. I thought you were referring to Bett Martin.'

'Good grief, no! That—! Oh, Miss Pink, how could you?'

'Who was it then?'

'Why, Nell Harvey, of course.' She went on quickly: 'It started soon after we came. It was quite innocent at first, they spent all their evenings climbing but then, in the autumn, they stopped climbing. . . . Of course, I knew there was something because he didn't come home till long after dark and he couldn't pretend he was climbing in the dark. He said he'd been drinking but he couldn't have been, I mean, he doesn't drink much and he'd have been incapable if he'd been in a pub all those hours. It was my fault. I had the evenings alone to write my book, you see. I liked being alone. I drove him to her.'

'I thought Joe was her climbing partner, not Jim.'

'Oh, it was Joe at weekends and holidays, but Jim in the evenings.'

Miss Pink drove away from the Lithgow cottage slowly and thoughtfully and she arrived back at the Centre still puzzling over Linda's careful revelations which were so different from her faltering but spontaneous disclosures of yesterday.

The common room was the old morning room at Plas Mawr and, at eleven o'clock, the sun had just topped the long spur of

Craig Wen. The room was at the south-east corner of the building with windows on two sides. Through these the brilliant light streamed in on a wide red carpet, on a huge shabby sofa where Ted lounged, relaxed, on easy chairs, a roaring fire. There was a smell of hot wood from logs steaming on the hearth, and of coffee. Miss Pink accepted a cup from Nell Harvey and studied the girl keenly. She looked, as always, neat and competent, but definitely not a *femme fatale*. This morning she wore tailored beige slacks and an ivory sweater. It appeared that she had been lecturing her own and Lithgow's patrols while he accompanied Hughes canoe-ing on the estuary.

'What was your subject?' Miss Pink asked.

'Erosion.'

The older woman smiled with sympathy.

'How do you cover that in one period?'

'Yes,' Nell said with emphasis, 'we must have more time for the environment.'

'Specifically? Do you mean at the Centre?'

'Yes. We have three periods. What can you teach them about world problems in three periods?'

'They aren't your concern,' Ted put in, 'today it was erosion.'

Nell turned to him. 'The Sahara advances ten miles in a year in places,' she said, 'if you cut down tropical forests the soil erodes because it won't grow crops. In Vietnam—'

'Not Vietnam,' Miss Pink said firmly, 'you can't carry the world on your shoulders, Nell. You must be satisfied with doing a worthwhile job in your own particular corner. I'm sure you make all the students aware of their immediate environment, and you're helping to equip them—'

'I wasn't going to mention napalm and burning babies,' Nell said, turning her cool eyes on Miss Pink, 'we were talking about erosion. After defoliation there will be no soil left in Vietnam. It's a world problem—erosion.'

'It seemed to be becoming rather emotional,' Miss Pink murmured.

51

'No, I wasn't emotional.'

That's true, Miss Pink thought. She doesn't get red-faced or weepy with frustration at the rate the oil is being used up, or about sewage in estuaries and fluoride.... Aloud she said wonderingly: 'You don't worry about problems like this, and pollution and over-population?'

Nell smiled. 'Do you really believe that man is the only animal that can't adjust his numbers to the available resources?'

'But,' Miss Pink floundered, 'you're not a conservationist then?'

'You mean: conserving water and minerals and fossil fuels. Yes, I suppose I am. One mustn't squander resources.'

'But you're not worried?' Miss Pink pressed, thinking that Nell was not very intelligent after all, remembering Linda's fierce concern with social justice, 'you think everything will come right on its own?'

'Not quite on its own. We'll have to pull our weight.'

'How?'

'Form pressure groups, lobby our M.P.s.'

Miss Pink knew that she was being made fun of. Not sure of her motives for doing so, she retaliated. 'Did you know that climber who did the Eiger in winter—Cary Paterson, was it?'

Nell's face set.

'Yes,' she said, and waited.

'Why did he kill himself?'

'I don't know.'

Ted said: 'Didn't he leave a note saying he took his life because he couldn't bear what people were doing to the world?'

There were voices outside in the hall. Miss Pink ignored them. 'Was that it?' she asked Nell.

The girl said gently: 'Cary wasn't a very strong character.'

Someone knocked. Nell went to the door and opened it. A small man in a raincoat stood there. He had a face like a sad ferret and Miss Pink might have thought him a commercial traveller but for the length of his raincoat. He introduced himself as Detective-Superintendent Crichton and they caught the initials "C.I.D." He sat down and Nell brought him a coffee.

The directors waited politely. Their faces gave nothing away but Miss Pink felt a *frisson* of trepidation. There was trouble here, but from which direction? An accident to Bett Martin? But they would send a uniformed man for that, or telephone. . . .

'Are you from London?' she inquired pleasantly, to break the silence as the little man sipped his coffee. 'Have you come all this way to ask us questions?'

'We have regional branches, madam.' He sounded like a shoe salesman. 'But in fact they've run into a little trouble in the old slate mines. Some of the explosives— Are you always here, madam?' he asked suddenly.

'No,' she said, 'I'm visiting.'

Ted took it upon himself to explain the situation and the directors' relationship with the Centre. The man appeared to lose interest in him and turned to Nell: 'How long have you been here, miss?'

'About two years.'

'And you're around the place all the time?'

'Most of the time I'm out.'

'Where?'

'On the hill, or canoe-ing.'

'On which hill?'

'None in particular.'

Miss Pink interposed: ' "On the hill" is an expression, Superintendent; it means simply "mountaineering".'

He glanced in her direction, acknowledged the interruption with a nod, and turned back to Nell: 'Ever go out at night?'

'Yes.'

'I mean, "on the hill".'

'Occasionally we have night expeditions.'

'In the combe where the mines are?'

'There are mines everywhere.'

'The one where the main entrance is. Cwm Caseg, is it?

'Not really. We don't use that one.'

'Where do you go?'

She started to elaborate with a list of Welsh place-names but he stopped her.

'That means nothing to me. D'you go anywhere that you can see into this Cwm Caseg?'

'Yes.'

'Ever see anything curious there, or hear anything?'

'Well, how curious?'

'Lorries, on that road up to the mine?'

'Well, there are Lawsons' lorries going up with loads. . .

'By night, I mean. See anything at night?'

'I can't remember,' Nell said, showing annoyance now, 'it's not always good weather; we're often in cloud high up.' She glanced at him with faint contempt. 'You've got enough to do in your own immediate vicinity. . . . If you saw lights, headlights, you'd assume that it was a couple who wanted privacy. Country roads are used for that purpose.'

'What are the lorries supposed to be doing?' Ted asked.

'No!' Miss Pink exclaimed unexpectedly, 'they couldn't have got into the mine!'

'They've got in all right,' Crichton said.

'Who?' Nell asked.

He didn't answer her.

'How much?' This from Ted.

'A fair amount, sir.'

'But—lorries in the plural,' Miss Pink exclaimed. 'That must have involved tons!'

'Oh yes, indeed, madam. Not just one lorry. A string of 'em. About twenty, I should say.'

'If one lorry carries three tons, that's sixty tons of gelignite, or whatever it is, that's missing,' Miss Pink said as they drove away from Plas Mawr.

'There are heavier vehicles than three-tonners,' Ted pointed out.

'All those bombs in Ireland. No wonder they've got plenty of explosives. But surely Lawsons are badly at fault. There couldn't have been any security at all.'

'They're still working on that. But as Crichton says, it could be an inside job. If one of the storemen is missing, it's pretty conclusive. However, you can't blame Lawsons for the defection of one of its employees. It happens everywhere.'

'What worries me is the thought of that convoy driving through the night with inadequate safety precautions. Suppose any one of them was involved in an accident as they went through an urban area. They could have blown up a whole town!'

'That's a point. How did they do it?'

'Do what exactly?'

'What kind of lorries would they use? You don't have convoys in peace time.'

'The Army still travels in convoys.'

He said nothing. A lay-by appeared. He drove off the road, stopped and turned to her.

'Yes,' she said before he could speak, 'it's the only way, isn't it? And who'd suspect them—a large number of Army vehicles? Their engines and tyres have a distinctive sound. No one would even trouble to look out of the window.'

'Where would they get the vehicles?'

'Any organisation that's big enough to steal tons of explosives at a time could command a string of service vehicles, however they obtained them in the first place. The problem in a country of this size is: where would they store them when they weren't in use?'

'Remote farms? Caverns?'

'It gets bigger,' Miss Pink shivered, 'It's frightening.'

'The only consolation is that they won't be able to do it again, now that the stuff's being evacuated. And they've got the Army guarding the mine entrance so no one will try any funny business.'

'About the Army,' she began as he reached for the ignition..

'Yes?'

She told him of the man who had blocked her vision when she was watching the soldiers climbing on the crag.

'Did he appear to do it deliberately?'

'Difficult to say. Surely it doesn't take a moment to pass in front of someone but I have the impression that he didn't start to move aside until I lowered the glasses. I mean, he did appear to pause: to block me deliberately.'

'Did you notice anything interesting about the chaps climbing?'

'Interesting, yes, but not unexpected.'

'We'll ask the Centre about them. As the rescue co-ordinator Lithgow's informed when another organisation comes to the area. I wonder. What else is there near the crag? I mean, that you might be taking an interest in?'

'Nothing really. Lithgow's cottage but that's at right-angles, away to the left—no, it isn't, it's almost in a direct line.' She closed her eyes, visualising the scene. 'There are the woods of course, either side of the ramp; scree, the mine—'

She stopped and they stared at each other in excitement. Then she relaxed.

'No good; it's the wrong side of the mountain—' She tailed off.

'Not that so much; the tunnels run for miles underground but in this particular case that's the way to the bricked-up level, remember?'

Many years before, a group of pot-holers had been exploring the old levels and had discovered a passage which connected with the explosives store. When they reported their find they were asked to seal off the passage which they did one weekend under the supervision of a police inspector from South Wales who had done some pot-holing himself.

'That's the other way in, is it? I never knew.' Miss Pink thought about this new angle. 'If it was only *bricked* up. . . .'

'That had occurred to me. A small explosive charge could be child's play to an expert.'

'But the police know all this. It's the first place they'd have thought of.'

'Police come and go. Records disappear, particularly after eighteen years.'

He started the engine and drove for some way in silence. Miss Pink stared out of the near window in the direction of the crag and the old mine entrance, neither of which was visible from this point.

'You want to go and see, don't you?' he asked.

'Yes. The more I think about that man, the more convinced I am that he was edging me away from the spot. And they left early, before lunch. Service units usually carry on with their exercise despite bad weather.'

Chapter Six

A TRACK SURFACED with chippings led to the camp site and Ted parked the car where the lorries had stood. Across the fields they could see a gable end of the Lithgow's cottage.

They had stopped at the Goat to pick up a packed lunch and two torches. Now Miss Pink selected a sandwich and said thoughtfully:

'The explosives business drove it out of my mind—but Linda appears convinced that Jim is having an affair, or has just finished one.'

'Does that concern us?'

'She says it's Nell.'

Ted chuckled. 'No!'

'I thought that too. Yesterday, when she told me without actually naming the woman, I thought she was referring to Bett Martin.'

'We-ll... Bett's not discriminating, but I can't imagine Lithgow.... He's a climber.'

'No time for it, d'you mean?'

'Quite. Same as Nell. They're at the age when, if they're not working, they live only for climbing. If they're not actually *on* rock, they do nothing else but talk about it among themselves: the next climb, the next alpine trip. You know; you've done it too.'

'I was never a tiger,' Miss Pink said modestly, 'the traverse of the Weisshorn was my limit; but I know what you mean. I thought it didn't fit. Jim has a strong sense of melodrama, would you say?'

'Ha! Teasing her, d'you think? Not very kind.'

'I don't think kindness is one of Jim's strong suits. Yes, it had crossed my mind that what she told me this morning was

58

rehearsed: a rehearsed retraction of what she said yesterday. She couldn't deny the story but she could change the characters—or rather, one of them. I think Jim might have insisted on that but I don't understand why he should substitute Nell. It seems a wild choice. Why weren't you surprised at the possibility of Bett Martin having an affair? Do you accept her husband's comments without question?'

'She's a slut,' he said shortly.

'It's not obvious.'

'Isn't it?'

'No. I would have said she was desperately bored and that she flirted as a diversion.'

'No, she doesn't flirt.'

She nodded, reflecting that he would know more of the local gossip than herself. She said wryly: 'Is it a coincidence that John managed to delegate power to us and escape to the States just as we have our first scandal?'

'—And the explosives blow up—in a manner of speaking? It must be a coincidence. John isn't that wily.'

She looked absently at the grassy ramp leading to the mine entrance: a blank black hole in the mountain-side.

'I don't like it,' she said.

'Rather go back?'

'No, I don't mean that. The mine doesn't bother me; I'm not claustrophobic. No, it's this business of the Martins. I have to keep reminding myself that the woman's *disappeared*. We all assume that she's gone away with a man but isn't that merely because it's the easy way out for us?'

'What are you suggesting?'

'I can't forget John saying on the phone that it would be as well if she didn't come back. There's a strong vein of callousness in this business.'

She had never been inside a mine and at first she was distracted by the speed with which Ted moved. Their torches were on headbands like miner's lamps. If she directed the beam downwards to see the ground, she was afraid of bumping her head on

59

the low ceiling. If she looked up in order to gauge the height, every nerve screamed that the next step would be into space.

Deep in the mine the sweating walls were shored with ancient props covered by a white fungus. The air felt warm but in places there were cool spots like cold patches in the sea. It was very quiet, but once, when they stopped and Ted was peering along a side tunnel, they heard a faint sound, unidentifiable.

'What's that?' she whispered.

'Bats.'

'*Bats!* We're too far inside!'

He didn't answer.

They came to flights of descending steps with thick, rust-flaked cables for handrails. Here their voices, which had bounced back stonily at them in the narrow passages, floated away into emptiness and she felt that they were surrounded by limitless fathoms of air. The torch beams were lost in it.

They started down one of these flights, one that was longer than the others. The steps were in the form of a zig-zag; they came to a square slate ledge and then turned back so that they were below the previous flight.

'Stop there,' Ted said suddenly.

She could see nothing beyond him because his body blocked her vision. She looked sideways over the edge where there was no rail. Her eyes widened and she flattened herself against the rock wall, tightening her grip on the cable. Water gleamed an incredible distance below.

'There's a break here,' he was saying, 'looks as if there's been a rock-fall. We can still get by though. What's left seems sound, but wait till I've crossed.'

Shining her torch on his feet she saw that the outer edge of the steps had gone, leaving a jagged break. He kicked each half-tread from the one above before he trusted his weight on it. The cable was still secure and he used this as a handhold. It looked to Miss Pink, as the gap widened between them, as if he were descending the wall of a monstrous well.

He stopped and turned to face her, standing easily.

'I'm across,' he called, 'it's not so bad as it looks. You can trust the cable.'

Her hands were sweating and she wiped them on her breeches, then she bent one stiff knee and kicked the first broken tread—but only the first. It was unnecessary, she chided herself; she had watched him test all the footholds. But the unique situation, so different from rock climbing, was disorientating; the dark water so far below, now invisible but *there*, the thick silence, the stillness, these spawned an irrational panic which she had never known in the open air.

She shook herself mentally and, with an enormous effort of will, concentrated on the next few feet of rock, and on the cable which was her life-line. She had to shine her torch downwards to make sure she didn't put her weight too close to the edge of the crumbling steps but, frowning with the effort, she refused to entertain any thought of what lay below that pool of light. Her spectacles steamed up and she swore.

'You're there,' Ted said calmly, and she saw the first whole step on the other side.

She followed him carefully to the bottom of the flight and some safe level place where she leaned against a wall and cleaned her spectacles.

'What's that water below?' she asked.

'They call it a loom. It's a catchment tank for floodwater.'

'How deep is it?'

'Deep enough,' he said grimly, 'but don't worry, we'll get back all right. It'll be easier going upwards.'

They started down another passage. At one point he stopped and she saw a hole in the wall about a yard wide and two feet high. It looked as if it might have been made by some projectile. Through the hole and against ubiquitous blackness their lights showed huge unstable slabs piled at bizarre angles.

'That's fresh,' he said.

'*Fresh?*'

'It wasn't there when I was a boy. Nor was the rock-fall on the steps, of course. The whole place seems to be disintegrating.'

'You have a fantastic memory. Is it good enough to find our way back?'

'Oh yes. I often came here with my uncle. He was manager—Mathias Roberts. He knew every yard of the levels and he loved the place—perhaps he hoped I'd come into the mine when I left school. But slate wasn't a career for me. The mine was just fun. I knew the levels pretty well in those days and you don't forget what you did when you were young. I'm remembering more as I go along.'

'And what's this hole?'

'Just the wall's collapsed.'

'But what's that *space* on the other side?'

'Why the next level down, I suppose.'

'It couldn't be one of those looms, could it?'

'That's quite possible, yes.'

They came to what appeared to be a dead end: a pile of rocks where the roof had fallen in. But in one corner of the mass there was an opening big enough to squeeze through.

'Look,' he said.

In the light she saw the marks of cleated boots in the mud. Instinctively she looked behind her, her light swinging over the walls and rotting timbers. She turned to Ted but he was starting to worm his way through the hole. In her torch beam a huge boulder which roofed the hole moved slightly. She opened her mouth to call him back but with a sudden scrabble his boots disappeared. She stared at the boulder dumbly.

'Right, come on. It's not too tight a squeeze.' His voice came distantly.

'Ted!'

'What? What's that?'

'This boulder moved. The one above the hole.'

'Oh. Did it. How much?'

'Very slightly. But I think it's jammed.' She was stooping, examining its edges. Among the surrounding rubble it was difficult to see where one rock ended and the next began.

'Oh damn,' she muttered, and aloud: 'I'll have to risk it. I'm coming through.'

She lay down gingerly and started to work forward. She was underneath the pile of rocks and could see Ted's light a few feet away when, holding her breath for another wriggle, she felt something light drop on her back. She gave a convulsive heave on her elbows, her fingers clawed slime—and a hand gripped her under the shoulder.

'Oh, my God,' she gasped as he helped her up, 'This is appalling!'

'Yes,' he said absently.

She recovered her breath and then, seeing what he was doing, joined him in directing her beam outwards.

They could see nothing at eye level but in front of their feet an uneven floor faded into infinity.

'It's the old face,' he told her, 'where they were working when the mine closed. It's a cavern.'

She followed him through a strange place of fallen rock and occasional level stretches where she tripped over small-scale railway lines. Once he stopped and showed her a chain of little trucks loaded with slate slabs: the last load.

They came to the now familiar entrance that marked the start of another level. After they'd gone a few yards there was a gleam of red on the fringe of her light.

'Here's a brick,' she said, 'several. They're *stacked*!'

They stopped and shone their lights ahead.

It was neat and colourful and totally incongruous: the remains of a brick wall which had blocked the way completely but now, with a large hole in the middle, it was merely a brick arch.

The return seemed interminable because it was difficult to talk while they were moving in single file. They had decided to go back the same way partly because this was quicker, but also because they envisaged complications and possibly even danger if the first people they encountered on the way to the main exit should be armed young soldiers over-sensitive to the sinister atmosphere of the place.

As they plodded through the tunnels Miss Pink's mind was

full of questions. Were those lorries loaded with gelignite when she passed the camp site yesterday morning? Was someone just emerging from the mine entrance when the guard—for that was surely what he was—stepped in front of her? Where had they come from? What story had they given the Centre to account for their presence in the valley?

They crossed the floor of the great cavern and crawled through the rock-fall without incident, almost without her noticing. After more passages steps appeared. She started to climb, reaching automatically for the handrail. She bumped into Ted. They both apologised.

'It's the break,' he said, 'above the loom.'

She waited while he crossed. In the loaded silence she heard a slight grating noise above. She looked up, her light sweeping the wall. Shadows loomed and leapt and something pale moved back from the edge of the light. There was a flutter like a bird's wings and she held her breath. From far below came a faint splash.

'Right,' Ted said, 'come on.'

She glanced up again, looking for something that wasn't a shadow but nothing moved.

She climbed across carefully, concentrating less on her footing than on what she might hear from above. A climber on steep rock is never sure what may come down but Miss Pink had the feeling that she had more than natural hazards to contend with at this moment.

'There's someone above us,' she whispered as she joined him, and told him about the falling stone.

'Did you actually see anyone?'

'No, only an impression of movement; of something, someone, dodging back from the light.'

'It's a sinister place,' he said, 'I used to imagine all kinds of things.

'We'll take it carefully,' she insisted, 'and we'll keep close together.'

But nothing untoward occurred and when they came to the

64

mouth of the mine and stood blinking in the sunshine, the woods below appeared empty and guileless.

'There's someone in the mine,' she repeated with emphasis.

'It's rats.'

'What would they live on—down there?'

They were moving down the ramp now and the sun was warm on their faces.

'The odd body perhaps?' he speculated cheerfully.

She glanced at him in reproof. The remark was in poor taste. He wouldn't have made it above the loom, she thought, and then paused. Had she been mistaken? Had it been a rat, or could the stone have fallen from some natural cause? You didn't have frost underground but perhaps they'd disturbed it as they descended and it had lain precariously on the edge until something, a current of air, a vibration, unbalanced it. Then what moved when she looked up? Or had that, after all, been imagination? Speculation was fruitless. Firmly she blocked out the incident and concentrated on the present.

They went to the Lithgows' cottage to telephone the police but the house was unoccupied and locked. They considered returning to the hotel but decided on reflection that there was no urgency. The explosives were gone and it could be only a matter of hours before the police discovered the means of access themselves.

The directors' original intention had been to see the canoe expedition come in to the estuary and they saw no reason for cancelling this, but since their way lay through the village of Bontddu, they did make the gesture of stopping at the police station there and trying to find Superintendent Crichton. They were told he was on the road, returning from county headquarters and could not be contacted. They left a message saying they would telephone him that evening and they continued to the estuary.

The sun was low on the water as they drove down a road parallel with the river.

'I thought the sea trips were finished for the season,' she remarked.

'The calm weather must have been too much of a temptation for Jim and, after all, they have the safety boat.'

'It can't prevent a ducking, only pick them out of the water—and the sea's pretty cold at this time of year.'

'No colder than the river.'

'But much farther to go before you can get a hot bath and a change of clothes. No, I don't like it. I've no desire to have the coroner asking me if I thought it wise to send children to sea in canoes in winter time.'

'Hallo,' he said, not listening to her, 'what have we here?'

A wooden slip ran down to the water and at the top there was an open space where a Mini van and the Centre's Land Rover were parked. A canoe trailer was coupled to the 'Rover which was jacked up on three wheels. Slade was stooping over the fourth, examining it. He looked up at their approach. He appeared annoyed but Miss Pink reflected that he never looked pleased to see anyone, except Nell.

'Slow puncture,' he said sullenly as Ted stopped beside him.

'Is the spare all right?'

'I think so. I was just looking to find a nail or something but I can't see anything so it must be a slow. I was pumping it up last week.'

Miss Pink stared at him. He was on the defensive. She left the car and Ted moved on to park it. Slade was taking the spare wheel off the 'Rover's bonnet. She glanced from the Mini to the Centre's vehicle.

'I see,' she said slowly, 'two of you drove to Porth Bach to pick up the Land Rover and trailer, and now Nell's going to drive you back to the Centre.'

'Not her. Wright.'

'Where is he?'

'He sloped off while I was changing the wheel. He wouldn't be any help.'

Ted came up, glancing seawards at a cluster of specks on the water.

66

'They're coming in,' he said, 'better drop that wheel at the garage as you pass, Joe, and see if they've got one to lend you. We can't afford to have the 'Rover off the road.'

'Yes, sir.'

Miss Pink's eyebrows rose a fraction.

'What happened to your patrol this afternoon—and to Wright's?' she asked.

'She's got them all on B.O.D.s—' he glanced at Ted who nodded. Biological Oxygen Demand was a test to assess the oxygen content of streams. He turned back to the wheel nuts. 'We had to leave our lads and come here because the canoe people would've been without transport else, and she said if they was wet, we'd got to get them back quickly.'

'She?' Miss Pink repeated pointedly.

'Nell.' He was awkward and belligerent and she realised that he had a curious reluctance to pronounce the name.

'The programme's a bit disrupted today,' Ted said agreeably. Slade glanced sideways at him. 'I take it you've been questioned by the detective?'

'Yeah. He questioned all of us.'

'But surely Hughes and Lithgow were on the water,' Miss Pink said.

'I mean, all of us at Plas.'

'Could you help them?'

'No, sir.'

'What do you know about the Army?' Miss Pink asked.

He gave a powerful twist to the last wheel nut and she sighed; unscrewing wheel nuts always gave her trouble.

'I don't know anything about the Army,' he answered. He threw the wrench in the back of the Land Rover. 'Wright!' he shouted suddenly.

'In a hurry to get back?' Ted asked.

'We've got enough on,' the man grumbled, rolling the spare wheel towards the Mini, 'lost a lot of time this afternoon, and she'll want the van.'

Paul Wright came up from the direction of the shore and greeted them. He looked inquiringly at Slade.

67

'Got to get back,' the man called. Wright smiled easily.

'Such a worker,' he observed to the directors in gentle mockery, 'I've been watching some ducks. Little black and white fellows.'

'Goldeneye,' Miss Pink said absently, 'Have you been down here long?'

'Most of the afternoon. It's high time we were back. That detective has messed up the routine. Funny chap; hasn't a clue, has he? As if you'd notice anything odd going on in the cwm, from the ridge, and at night! And what are the odds that they came on the particular night that we happened to be up there?'

'But they didn't—' she began, to find herself over-ridden by Ted: 'I understand the police were after any curious happenings anywhere in the locality, not confined to Cwm Caseg. There are other entrances to the mines.'

'Are there?' Wright's interest was obvious. 'You don't mean— but surely there can't be other means of access to the *explosives*? That's impossible. Or outrageous,' he added as an afterthought.

'There was,' Ted told him, 'but it was sealed off.'

He related the story of the pot-holers' discovery but didn't mention their own adventure that afternoon.

Wright said with amusement: 'You know, if someone unblocked that passage it would be a far more reasonable way of getting the stuff out than using the main entrance, unless of course, they had inside help for the job.'

Slade, tired of waiting, had started the Mini and was now sitting stolidly behind the wheel with the engine running. Beside Wright's pleasant manner, his behaviour was oafish. The young man raised his eyebrows helplessly, took his leave, and the van left with a spurt of gravel.

'Slade *is* uncouth,' she observed, 'it's amusing how he defers to Nell though.'

'He gets along with most of the boys,' Ted commented. 'Not with the sensitive ones, of course.'

'I think Paul copes with him.'

'Yes, that lad's not quite so ingenuous as he appears. And

68

he caught on to the significance of the alternative entrance immediately, didn't he?'

'Well, it's so obvious when you know there was once another way to the store. It was an opportunity waiting to be exploited.' She looked pleased with her choice of words.

The canoes were close now, their wheeling paddles catching the last of the sunlight. Accompanying them, but at a distance, the safety boat chugged softly through the water.

'Very pretty,' Ted remarked, 'and all going well.'

With a sudden increase of engine noise the safety boat circled round the canoes and headed for the slip. They walked down to meet it. Jim Lithgow cut the engine and handed Ted the painter, then he stepped ashore.

'Been waiting long?' he asked, not looking at them.

'Not long. Have a good trip?'

'Reasonable for the time of year.' He surveyed the approaching canoes. He didn't comment on the Mini being so long in the car park.

'We've had the C.I.D. at the Centre,' Miss Pink said.

He turned then, his eyes like broken glass in the sun.

'They've discovered that a lot of the explosives are missing,' Ted added.

'Why did they come to us?'

Miss Pink explained. By this time Hughes and the boys were coming in to the slip and the directors and the chief instructor moved up to the river bank. Hughes stared after them until the horseplay of the boys coming ashore recalled him to his duty.

'Don't people who come to climb in the area inform you beforehand?' Miss Pink asked Lithgow.

'Only if they're in a group. Not individuals.'

'What was the unit at the camp site this weekend?'

'I'm not sure.'

'But there'll be a record at the Centre?'

'We don't always write it down.'

There was a heavy silence.

69

'But as rescue co-ordinator,' Ted said, 'shouldn't you know who's operating in your area?'

'Not necessarily. We know who they are if something happens to them and we're called out, of course. Not much point if there's no accident.'

'Not to keep track of what's happening?' Ted urged.

Lithgow shrugged, then thought better of it.

'Someone will know,' he said, 'they'll have rung the Centre before they came. Sally will know—or Nell.'

Contacted by telephone from the Goat neither Sally nor Nell knew anything about the Army unit. They had a record of most organisations that camped in the valley but this one appeared to have come and gone without recording its presence or attracting attention. Feeling tired, Miss Pink relinquished the telephone to Ted, leaving him to report their discovery in the mine to Crichton.

She repaired to the lounge where he found her some time later with not only two glasses, but a bottle of Tio Pepe in front of her. She poured him a drink which he accepted with gratitude.

'None of the storemen is missing,' he said as he sat down, 'so apparently it wasn't an inside job, but here's something significant: an Army unit in the Midlands reported four of its vehicles stolen some time on Friday night!'

'Four isn't enough for the amount of explosives stolen.'

'It would be if several units each reported a batch of missing vehicles. Or it could have been done in instalments, over a period.'

'Stealing a few lorries at a time? Surely that would be giving the game away—and if *our* lorries on the camp site were the stolen Midland ones, where are they now?'

'Yes, Crichton is very interested in those and wasn't at all happy when I told him that there was no record of them at the Centre. I'll bet the wires are humming to the local bobbies at this moment as he tries to find out how the military operates

70

in an area without their knowledge—that is, assuming they didn't leave any trace.'

'What did he say about the break-in at the mine?'

'Astounded firstly, then angry, finally philosophical. He mentioned the horse and the stable door, but he's putting a strong guard up there and they'll have to seal off that level again. There's a tremendous amount of stuff in the mountain; it will take weeks to evacuate. They're starting tomorrow.'

'I hope that means we've seen the last of it.'

'Yes, it's someone else's pigeon now: both the stuff that's gone, and what's going to be removed legally.'

He dined at the Goat as her guest. It was an excellent meal since the kitchen knew well in advance and Miss Pink had approved the menu without change except to delete the pudding. It was *tournedos à la Béarnaise*.

The beef was tender and the Stilton couldn't have been better, he told her, had she chosen it. Two elderly gourmets, they leaned back from their good coffee and smiled at each other. They were both tired but now they could relax. At that moment Olwen came trotting down the dining room and Miss Pink frowned. They were in need of nothing, least of all more shreds of village gossip, but she felt a rising thrill of anticipation for Olwen's face was alight with excitement.

The blue Jaguar had been found.

71

Chapter Seven

LEFT ALONE WHILE Ted telephoned the police for confirmation, Miss Pink felt deflated. Olwen didn't know where the car had been abandoned, but that seemed unimportant. They had been pretty sure what had happened; this was an anti-climax.

Ted was a long time on the telephone and when he returned she regarded him with a trace of annoyance which passed as she realised that he was puzzled.

A car was lying on its side below the cliffs west of Puffin Cove. At low water the first three letters of its registration, JCA, were visible. Although the make wasn't known, it was pale blue—and the registration of Martin's car was JCA. Because it had been submerged at least since Sunday afternoon there was no possibility of any occupants being alive, so frogmen would not be going down until tomorrow morning.

The car was first sighted on Sunday afternoon by—here Ted looked at the back of an envelope—a Mrs Wolkoff who lived at Porth Bach, which lay about half a mile east of Puffin Cove. She had assumed that it was scrap and that the owner had been trying to dispose of it, so on Monday morning she telephoned the public health inspector to lodge a complaint. Since she was well known in the council offices for her public-spirited behaviour her protest was treated as routine and shelved until someone should have the time and energy to deal with it.

However, after another visit to the scene and perhaps incensed that nothing was being done to recover the wreck, she telephoned the public health department again and said that she was wondering if the car had been stolen. The inspector's assistant dissuaded her from informing the police, privately convinced that the suggestion that the car was stolen was merely a gambit to get it moved. It wasn't until seven o'clock this evening that the inspector, meeting the traffic superintendent in the local sailing club, chanced to mention Mrs Wolkoff's latest protest. Evidently the lady was known to departments other than Public Health.

The superintendent happened to be one of the people whom Ted had contacted on Sunday afternoon in respect of the missing Jaguar, and the coincidence of both colour and registration was enough to send the police down to Puffin Cove, but since it was high water nothing could be determined even with the aid of a portable searchlight, and further investigations were abandoned till daylight.

'I don't think that there's any doubt that it's the right car,' Ted said.

'What could she have been doing down there?'

'We don't know that she was there. Perhaps she drove to a rendezvous, got into a car driven by someone else, abandoned the Jaguar and it was stolen later. Saturday night's a good time for stealing cars.'

But they both saw the snag while he was speaking. No car thief or midnight reveller would steal a vehicle to abandon it on a remote and uninhabited stretch of coast.

'Could it be,' Miss Pink suggested, 'that Puffin Cove was where "X" picked her up—no, he'd have met her close to the main road, or at least nearer to the school, not so far from Plas Mawr. And if that were the case, they'd never have driven miles out of their way in two cars just to abandon the Jaguar. That doesn't make sense.'

They were both avoiding the thought that was uppermost in their minds. Their eyes met and it only remained for one to say it.

'You think she's in it, don't you?' she asked.

'I'm afraid so.'

'Yes,' she sighed, 'so all the rest is speculation: the how and why. I suppose there will be some indication ... they seem to be able to find out anything nowadays, although—' her voice

73

sharpened, 'I would like to know what she was doing down there.'

At ten o'clock the following morning they left the Goat and drove to Porth Bach in Ted's car. The first four or five miles, down to the main road and along this westwards, parallel with the coast and about a mile inland, lay through flattish farmland. On their right was the line of mountains; to the left the sea and a fine rocky headland sheltering a bay on its eastern side.

After less than ten minutes a signpost pointed left to the Schooner Hotel and Porth Bach. They took this side road until about half a mile short of the headland where they turned left again along a narrow tarred track which was only wide enough for one vehicle. At intervals there were passing-places.

The road was unfenced and sometimes the ground dropped steeply from the grass verge to the top of the cliffs. There was a lot of gorse and dead bracken.

After two miles the road started to dip and Porth Bach appeared below them: a wooded ravine running down to a beach. The cove would have once housed a small fishing community. There was a landing place, and a jetty in moderately good repair. Ruins showed here and there but among the trees there were four stalwart cottages. Of these, only one chimney smoked; the others were closed and shuttered against the winter and vandals.

The road zig-zagged into the cove with a sharp angle between diagonals and ended above the jetty in a rough circle of mud and shingle where two police vehicles were parked: a car and a Land Rover with an empty trailer. A constable in uniform watched the approach of the newcomers phlegmatically.

Ted stopped on the turning-circle and cut his engine. It was quiet but for gnomish voices and pips from the police radio. The constable, having recognised Ted, said that there was no news. Frogmen were at the wreck now and the local inspector, Bowen, had persuaded Mr Dawson, the owner of the Schooner Hotel, to come along in his launch, so everyone was out on the water.

74

Miss Pink, sensing the idleness in the air and feeling super-fluous, moved down to the shore.

Two derelict boats lay above the jetty, but above the tide-line there was a varnished dinghy in good condition. At the other end of the short beach all that remained of some larger vessel was its timbers sticking up like a rib cage.

There was nothing to do here and she decided to walk along the top of the cliffs. Ted said he would pick her up if she didn't return before the—he hesitated—recovery party.

She walked back the way they had driven, pausing occa-sionally to study the scene. This was where the canoes had started from yesterday, but whereas the Jaguar (if it was the Jaguar) lay west of the cove, the Centre's party had paddled east.

She looked back as she strolled uphill and saw that Ted was now on the jetty. Inland, someone was standing at the open door of the occupied cottage: a slight figure in dark clothing partly obscured by a shrub, but from the rigid posture Miss Pink realised with amusement that she was being observed through binoculars. This must be Mrs Wolkoff unless, of course, that lady didn't live alone, but somehow the story of the finding of the car and subsequent events sounded like the behaviour of a solitary widow: someone trying to find a use for her time.

She reached level ground but instead of keeping to the tarmac she chose to walk along the true top of the cliffs where there was a narrow and, in places, hazardous path. Most of the time the road was on a higher level and occasionally as much as a hundred yards distant.

The sea was very calm except off the eastern headland where the surf broke silently. The nearer cliffs were about a hundred feet high, with a belt of golden lichen along their tops. The bare lower rock was black or red or almost white, sometimes firm with smooth faces, occasionally interspersed with rust-coloured intrusions that looked like vertical earth. A slight swell was running and at long intervals there came the sound of a distant watery explosion in the back of a cave.

There was no sign of either boat or wreck but since visibility

75

was restricted by a small jutting buttress ahead, a considerable stretch of coastline was hidden from her. Some distance away across the bay, the hotel shone white on the point. The good weather was holding and although it was mainly overcast, there were patches of sunlight on the water.

The path curved inland to skirt the top of the buttress which was itself the miniature headland of Puffin Cove. She took a few steps to the top of the rise and looked across the stretch of water that had been hidden before.

Below her lay the shallow cove which was little more than an indentation in the coastline. On the other side of it, about half a mile away, were two boats: the larger stationary some distance from the foot of the cliffs. There were figures in the stern. The smaller craft resembled the Centre's safety boat and was approaching the other from the direction of the cliffs. There were two people in this and she could hear its outboard motor.

The two craft merged for a few minutes, then the smaller boat detached itself and headed towards Porth Bach. Because it was so low in the water and she was a hundred feet above, she could look into it as it passed. Between the sinister figures of the crew in their gleaming wet suits there was a dark bundle with pale exposed flesh but she was too far away to see who it was.

She saw the launch come round and follow the frogmen and heard the soft throb of its engine below the urgent chatter of the outboard. She continued slowly, watching the ground, thinking, but automatically aware of stones and little breaks in the path that could cause a slip. She stopped suddenly, staring at the stamped earth.

There was the imprint of a tyre.

Obviously, she thought: there would be—but it brought the situation 'home to her more poignantly than the sight of the body. It was the question of distance: the mark was a few inches from the toe of her boot. There was only one imprint; the car would have been bouncing by the time it reached this point and only one wheel had touched. Elsewhere, tyres hadn't marked the turf but there were gouged scrapes in the slope and new white scratches on rock: all evidence of the car's passage when it plunged off the road.

She prospected along the cliffs until she found a place, some fifty yards away, from which she could look back and down to the spot immediately below the tracks. It was nearly high tide and she could see nothing under the surface. If it was high tide now, at eleven, it would have been high about eight on Saturday evening, low tide at two—but even at low water the Wolkoff woman had said that the car was all but submerged. The occupant had stood no chance.

She climbed up to the road and walked back until she could discover, by the marks below, where the Jaguar had left the tarmac. At that point there was a passing place on the seaward side of the road.

She was still staring at the short stretch of ground between road and cliff when Ted's car approached from Porth Bach. He stopped and Miss Pink looked a question.

'It's her,' he said, 'well, hardly any doubt.'

'Why should there be any?'

'Crabs. She's been there several days—and the window's open.'

She made a grimace of disgust, then said loudly, to distract them both:

'This must be the place where she left the road.'

'Is it?' He showed interest, and got out to study the marks.

'She must have been turning round and put her foot on the accelerator instead of the break,' he said. 'What a mad place to turn! She'd only to go another mile and she could turn in the cove.'

'Would she know that?'

They looked at each other. Neither knew the extent of Bett Martin's familiarity with the area. Ted frowned.

'What was she doing down here?' he muttered, walking away, staring at the turf on the other side of the road.

'This will be a popular site in summer,' he said, glancing at the gorse bushes. 'Couples at night, I suppose, and picnic parties in the daytime. There's a lot of litter.... I wonder if she parked here—and why.' He turned and looked at Miss Pink. 'She didn't have to come for the obvious reason,' he added.

'What else?' She was startled. 'But whatever she came for, it wasn't for something innocent. The choice of site confirms that. She didn't want to be seen. But she didn't come here alone.'

'She could have done. Perhaps the person she had an appointment with didn't turn up. She could have worked herself into a temper, waiting, and tried to turn round without thinking where she was. She could have been drunk.'

'What do the police think?'

'They're coming now. Let's see what they have to say.'

A car was approaching from Porth Bach. It stopped and Ted introduced Inspector Bowen, an unhappy white-haired man who looked as if he suffered from dyspepsia. Miss Pink remembered that, with Ted, she was representing the Board and her thoughts went off at a tangent as she wondered if there might be time to delay Beresford's flight to New York, but she knew she wouldn't contact him. The accident was sordid but simple and his advice would be to keep it as quiet as possible. She listened to Ted talking about the tracks.

The inspector hadn't seen them until that moment. He was more intrigued by the fact that the dead woman had been turning here than that she should have come down to the cliffs in the first place. He had no doubt it was to meet a man.

'No other explanation,' he said, 'she was the type, begging your pardon, miss.'

'Did you know her?' Miss Pink asked.

'No, but word gets around.'

Tactfully he offered no sympathy and it wasn't until he'd been driven away that she wondered why he'd said nothing about finding the man.

'Difficult,' Ted said. 'He certainly won't come forward. He's probably married and won't want to be compromised. We do know now that she wasn't intending to clear off; there was no luggage in the car.'

'He left her to drown,' she said grimly.

'She wouldn't have stood a chance. It would take too long

78

to get down the cliffs even if he were a climber, even if there was a feasible route. Did you see one?'

'There's no place where you could get down easily and quickly in the dark. You're right, but one would like to think he made some attempt to reach her—if there was a man. What did the divers find? Anything to indicate why she went over?'

'Not really. The driver's window was open, the car was in neutral gear.' He stopped and thought about this, then went on: 'It's lying on its side.'

'Were the doors open?'

'No. Jammed shut. They had to use a crowbar to get the body out.'

'I wonder why he was outside the car. I suppose he was directing her as she turned.'

They sat together behind the desk in the warden's office at Plas Mawr. They were divorced from each other by silence and their own thoughts. It was not so much that they were thinking along different lines, but similar ones. Something was wrong and neither of the directors cared to speculate on its nature.

The door opened and seven people filed in, awkwardly and all more or less self-conscious. There were the five instructors and Sally Hughes and Linda Lithgow. For a moment they didn't know what to do.

'Please sit down, and smoke if you wish,' Miss Pink said pleasantly. No one took advantage of her second offer.

It was curiously embarrassing to see them so uneasy, like schoolchildren called before the headmaster. Violent death had found the chink in their armour. They knew, of course; that was obvious.

Ted waited until they had found themselves chairs, then cleared his throat quietly.

'I think you know why we've called all the staff together,' he began, 'Mrs Martin has had an unfortunate accident—'

Miss Pink, appearing to stare vaguely at the assembly from behind her spectacles, was watching their faces intently. She saw horror, doubt, and frowns that indicated—what? Joe

Slade glared at the floor, Nell's face was set, her eyebrows raised a little giving her an air of whimsical surprise. Sally looked as if she might cry, Linda appeared angry as, indeed, did Rowland Hughes. Lithgow's eyes widened like those of a startled colt. Wright wiped his face with his hand and Miss Pink looked at him a little longer than the rest, thinking he appeared the most affected—but no, it had hit them all. It was the shock. In a climbing community one is constantly aware that one of the climbers may be killed; the fact that people also die, and more of them, in road accidents, is forgotten.

Ted finished speaking and there was a long silence. No one moved.

'Are there any questions?' he asked.

'It sounds heartless,' Sally said, 'but—how does this affect us? I mean, should we do anything?'

'I don't think any of you will need to attend the inquest,' he assured them, 'it's up to you, of course, what you do about the funeral—if it's held here. Martin will return and stay in the village—' Relief flickered across several faces. 'Where you will be affected and, indeed, the reason why we needed to see you together and formally, is in relation to the Press. They'll be around anyway this week as soon as they hear the explosives are being evacuated—the police haven't a hope of keeping *that* quiet. Miss Pink and I are concerned that no one should speak to reporters about our own particular trouble, but will refer them to ourselves. The matter isn't going to be hushed up, but for the sake of our work here it's better that the papers should have only one account of the accident, and that from the Board. Is that understood?'

His tone was even but held no possibility of dissent. There was an affirmative murmur. He thanked them and they filed out. Unlike children they didn't break into excited chatter as soon as the door was closed. No sound came from the hall. The directors looked at each other.

'Well,' he said, 'I suppose one wouldn't expect it to go any differently.'

'I think they were dumbfounded.'

'Odd, isn't it? She was asking for trouble: drinking, driving, then driving that particular car—and when it happens, they're shocked. Death, especially violent death, is never anticipated by youth. You're not surprised, are you?'

'No, but I'm puzzled. How long before we know the result of the post mortem?'

'I said I'd ring Llewelyn—he's the police surgeon—at five. Are you thinking of suicide?'

'I don't think anyone would set out to deliberately drown themselves that way but it's possible that she parked the car facing the sea, took a lot of pills, tranquillisers perhaps, and some drink, then after a while she took the handbrake off.'

Neither of them observed that Bett Martin had shown no suicidal tendencies to their knowledge. In fact, both were starting to be weary of the subject.

'Shall we go for a stroll?' he asked.

But she wanted to supervise the removal of Martin's furniture. Sally Hughes had found a van and it was coming at two o'clock.

'It seems heartless,' she said, 'handling that furniture now.'

'Got to be done. I'll help; we'll still have time to stretch our legs before I phone Llewelyn.'

By three o'clock the flat was empty, the furniture van gone and they set out for a quick walk round the head of the valley.

The sun was setting and the sky tinged with colour as they came out on top and saw the northern mountains with the snowfields a pale rose in the evening light. Neither was interested in the peaks. They both looked downwards, at the road which climbed to the mine.

Far below, rear lights showed where vehicles were descending and from close at hand they could hear the sound of engines. A dark shape with headlights blazing moved out of the mine compound. It was followed by two more, on side lights.

'Good gracious!' Miss Pink exclaimed, 'is that a lorry and two escort vehicles?'

'Yes, that's how they're doing it.'

'They are worried, aren't they?'

'I'm not,' he said morosely, 'not about *that.*'

'Yes. If the Press ask what we think she was doing down there, what line do we take?'

'I can think of nothing better than total ignorance.'

'And Martin's dismissal?'

'He resigned.'

'He resigned at an odd moment.'

'He did, didn't he?'

They started to retrace their steps, walking side by side down the wide path. Two ravens, homing late to their roost, came flapping up the slope to veer away with startled barks as they caught sight of the figures moving down the track in the gloaming.

It was Miss Pink who broke the silence.

'It can't have any significance.'

'No.'

She noted that although they hadn't spoken for some time he knew exactly what she meant.

The telephone rang in the secretary's office as Miss Pink was about to leave. She had gone into the Centre to say that they were back from the hill and could be found if needed that evening at the Goat. Ted was at that moment outside changing his boots. Miss Pink nodded goodbye to Sally and moved to the door as the phone rang. She moved more slowly as the secretary's voice rose sharply:

'Who? ... They're here now.... He's outside, but Miss Pink is with me....'

She turned back and saw that the girl's eyes stared at her too hard.

'Doctor Llewelyn,' Sally said, holding out the receiver.

Llewelyn was very Welsh. His excited voice crackled at speed. She turned her back on Sally, wishing with a corner of her consciousness that she could be mistaking what she was hearing, that Llewelyn was mistaken, but every word, every phrase illuminated the truth.

'Yes,' she said, 'I'll tell him.'

She replaced the receiver carefully.

'That was the post mortem report,' she said, 'she wasn't drowned. She was strangled.'

Horror and disbelief struggled in Sally's face. She moistened her lips.

'Shall I tell the others?' she whispered.

'I suppose so.' Miss Pink was moving towards the door again, anxious to see Ted. 'If they don't know already,' she added absently.

Chapter Eight

'IT'S NOT ENTIRELY unexpected,' Ted said.

They were sitting in the car. He'd made no move to drive away after hearing her news.

'It answers a lot of questions,' she agreed, 'the fact that the car should have been turned in such a dangerous place, that it was in neutral instead of bottom or reverse. . . . And I found it difficult to credit that anyone could even consider suicide in that manner. How could she hit on the exact moment to release the handbrake and yet be drowsy enough not to *mind* dying so horribly? When did you first think of murder?'

'It occurred to me this afternoon—definitely. But it had crossed my mind before that. Probably this morning when suicide seemed even more illogical than accident. But once you'd entertained the thought of suicide it was only a step to violence by a second person. What were the signs?'

'There was no water in the lungs and there were marks on the throat and—what's the hyoid?'

'Ah yes, that's a pretty sure sign. There was a case in Rhyl some years ago. It's a bone in the throat that gets fractured in strangling.'

'They're getting a pathologist down but Llewelyn seems to think that it's only a matter of confirmation. She'd also drunk a lot of whisky.'

He started the car. Glancing at the lighted windows as they drove past, she said: 'I feel as if we're abandoning them.'

'You'll be feeling the responsibility more than them,' he said, 'they're resilient; once they've got over the shock they'll soon be back to normal. It would be a different matter if she'd been popular.'

'If she'd been popular she wouldn't be dead,' she said tartly.

When they reached the Goat, Ted drove through the car park at the side of the building to the garage at the back. There were no cars visible other than Miss Pink's neat Austin.

'No Press or police,' he observed. 'I shall stay the night. We should both be on hand. Can they put me up, d'you think? The place seems very quiet. Where are the staff's cars?'

'Shippam—the manager—and his wife, are in Ibiza. Olwen is the only resident maid. I imagine she could call on some of the summer staff if necessary but otherwise there's only Miss Devereux and a barman and they don't come in till later.'

They went in the hotel. The fact that accident had become murder had not yet reached Olwen, probably due to the telephone system being automatic. In the old days someone on the grapevine would be related to the girl on the switchboard.

'A terrible thing,' she said, meeting them in the hall, 'that Betty Plas lying there since Saturday evening and no one knowing.'

'Terrible,' Ted agreed.

'We're very thirsty,' Miss Pink told her.

'I'll get you a pot of tea this minute. You'll have had a hard day, I'm sure.'

Out of regard for the carpets they stayed in the reception hall for Miss Pink was still wearing her walking boots and suddenly she felt too tired to go upstairs and change before drinking tea. She relaxed thankfully in an easy chair.

'Well,' she said, 'I suppose this is as bad as it can get.' Remembering that they were in a public place she lowered her voice. 'I'm worried about the staff.'

'At Plas Mawr?' She nodded. 'You know who the first suspect is—always?'

'The husband. But it's often manslaughter. If he'd known she was going to meet someone and followed her out there—'

'In what?'

'What?'

'She'd taken the Jaguar; how would Martin get to the coast?'

'Well!' she exclaimed happily, 'that puts him in the clear, doesn't it?'

Ted said nothing. She went on less happily: 'And after the husband come lovers—'

'And wives.'

'This is unpleasant,' she said.

'Yes, I know, so is murder.'

They were silent for a moment, then she said: 'Strangling must need an awful lot of strength.'

'Not when the victim's drunk.'

'She wouldn't have sat in the car drinking with a woman.'

'She could have been killed elsewhere.'

'Then you'd need an accomplice—if the murderer was someone from the Centre. You must have two drivers, not essential perhaps, but I can't see anyone walking back to the Centre after pushing the car over the cliffs; it must be a good eight miles. Did you notice tracks this morning when you were looking at the verge?'

'I wasn't looking specifically for tyre marks. In any case they wouldn't necessarily be associated with the murder; anyone could have parked there Saturday afternoon or since Saturday evening.'

Olwen brought their tea, clucking sympathetically but darting sharp glances at them, waiting for them to start talking again. They got rid of her but now, aware of doors that were ajar, they were circumspect, discussing guardedly whether and when they should return to Plas Mawr.

They were on their third cup of tea when the police arrived. They were strangers to her but she didn't have to look at Ted to know that they were police, and her heart beat unhealthily fast. She had time to reflect that even the innocent are touched with guilt where some crimes are concerned, then Ted was introducing a large man, somewhat pear-shaped, who moved lightly across the room towards them, bearing his paunch before him. He was almost bald and he had a shiny, rubbery face and a jovial manner which she felt he moderated now, probably because of her relationship with the Centre. Small eyes summed her up briefly. He was Detective Superintendent Pryce. She shook hands, distrusting him.

His sergeant was angular and in his thirties: a Williams. He had soft brown eyes and no chin. He looked ineffectual. She was sure he wasn't.

Olwen, hovering by the service door, was asked to bring more tea and scones. The newcomers removed their coats and sat down. Miss Pink felt ridiculous in her breeches and boots and wondered how soon she could escape.

The superintendent chattered about the Centre, about the enthusiasm of Sir Thomas for this and that, and the problem of juvenile delinquency; there was plenty to keep him going while Olwen made more tea. He waited until she'd served it, thanked her heartily, and leaned back. Miss Pink started to pour out in the ensuing silence. The atmosphere wasn't easy; she had to remind herself that Ted was on her side. She kept seeing the top of the cliff and the pale blue Jaguar going over, which was ridiculous because when it happened the colour wouldn't have shown.

'Where's the husband?' the superintendent asked suddenly.

'He left for London yesterday morning,' Ted told him.

'Leave a forwarding address?'

'I have it upstairs,' Miss Pink said, seizing her chance.

There was no time to bath. She slipped into a dress, determined to miss as little as possible, but Ted came upstairs as she left her room.

'He's bringing Martin back,' he told her, 'and they're going up to Plas Mawr. They've agreed to let us be present when they interview the staff. We'll not get any dinner tonight,' he ended unhappily.

'I'll ask Olwen to leave something for later. What's in their minds—interviewing?'

'To get a general picture, I would think, but mainly to try to find out what Martin was doing at the relevant time.'

87

'You didn't mention Linda's story?'

'No. If there's any truth in it, it will come out. I just sketched people in for him and answered questions. Better let him discover the situation for himself.'

The police saw the staff in the warden's office. They started with Sassie Owen who was frightened and truculent. She had little to add to what Olwen had told Miss Pink. It appeared that she had seen someone in the driver's seat of the Jaguar after she'd looked out of the window, attracted by the crashing gears.

'How could you tell it was a woman then?' the superintendent pressed, 'it could have been a man.'

'No, I saw her hands and legs, didn't I? The light shines out and I saw her rings. It's as bright as day out there, but I couldn't see above here,' she indicated her left hip.

'What time was this?'

'Just after seven. We were serving up. We start serving at seven.'

'You're quite sure that there was no one in the back of the car?'

'How do I know? Could have been. Right over on the other side. But I'd 'a seen his legs, wouldn't I?'

'I expect she was alone,' Pryce said when Sassie had gone, 'if someone wanted to keep out of the way he wouldn't have risked getting in the car down here. He'd have arranged to be picked up outside the Centre. I'd like to see the secretary next.' He looked uncertain; he couldn't give Ted the job of messenger boy.

'I'll tell her,' Miss Pink said. They demurred politely but she went.

Sally was in her office. She looked at her employer brightly but she was tense all the same.

'The classic case of "it always happens to someone else", isn't it?' she observed.

The superintendent looked very much at home behind the warden's desk; he was solid and conventional, the kind of man who might have shown some hint of disapproval had a hippie or tramp been shown in but Sally appeared to make a good impression. She was wearing a quiet dark dress with a ceramic pendant and no make-up except soft lipstick. She sat down and regarded him carefully.

The preliminaries over, Pryce asked her when she had last seen Martin. She blinked. The question had been unexpected.

'I shall have to think,' she said, excusing her silence.

'Take your time,' he told her comfortably. He looked idly along a shelf of books on the nearest wall.

'It must have been after Sunday lunch,' Sally said.

'Sunday,' he repeated heavily and his eyes flickered to the sergeant taking notes at the side of the desk. 'Perhaps you would explain the circumstances.'

'He was passing through the hall to the front door. He didn't speak.'

'Do you know what he did after that?'

Sally hesitated and it occurred to Miss Pink that Pryce knew only as much as Ted had time to tell him while she was changing.

'I don't *know* what he did, only what I've been told,' Sally said.

'Who saw him later than that? What was the time?'

'About half past one.'

'Well, of course, I did,' Miss Pink said.

'Ah.' He didn't follow this up but stayed with Sally: 'I understand Martin was duty instructor on Sunday.'

'Yes.'

'And that duty starts when?'

'At eight-thirty, after breakfast.'

'Can you tell me if he started at eight-thirty that morning?'

'No, because last weekend he had two consecutive duties: Saturday night and Sunday.'

'Is that usual: for the warden to be doing the work of an instructor?' He asked the question of the directors.

'No,' Ted said, 'but it's up to him. It will please his staff since their duties will come round less often.'

89

'When does the duty instructor start in the evening?'

'At five o'clock, which is the normal finishing time for inside activities if there's nothing happening in the evening.'

'So Martin came on duty at five o'clock on Saturday?' He'd turned back to Sally.

'No.'

'No,' he repeated. 'Why not?'

'He asked me to stand in for him that evening.'

'For how long?'

'I told him I would stay until ten-thirty.'

'What time did he relieve you?'

'About eleven.'

'How did he appear—what was his manner like?'

'He was drunk.'

'Then how could he go on duty?'

'I don't mean he was incapable. He had been drinking heavily.'

'Will you tell us how he came in?'

She looked puzzled.

'How he entered the building,' Pryce elaborated, 'did he appear to have come in from the front or the back?'

'Oh, he wasn't out. I had to go up to the flat. When he didn't appear by eleven I thought he might be upstairs although until then I'd assumed he'd gone out. I couldn't make him hear; he'd got the record player on rather loud, so I opened the door. He was lying on the sofa—asleep.'

'What did you do?'

'I went in and turned the record player down and woke him.'

'Had he been drinking?'

'There was a nearly empty whisky bottle beside him on the floor and a glass.'

'What did he say?'

'I told him the time and he apologised and sat up. He said he felt awful and probably I'd have offered to take his place for a while but I had to go home. I have a family. So he followed me downstairs although there was nothing to do. I'd put the lights out in the dormitories long before but I suppose he wanted to show he was fit to take over.'

'What did you do then?'

'I cycled home. Our car was off the road.'

There was a map on the desk in front of him.

'Would you show me where you live?' he asked.

Sally got up and showed him and he took a biro from his pocket, removed the cap and marked the place carefully.

'Now,' he said, leaning back and beaming at her, 'I won't keep you much longer. You saw Martin at eleven o'clock. When did you last see him before that?'

'I saw him on the stairs at tea time, about five o'clock.'

'Was that when he asked you to stand in for him?'

'No, he asked me that morning. He wasn't feeling well. He had a liver complaint.'

'So you didn't see him between five and eleven. Could he have left the building?'

'He could have,' she said slowly, 'I was all over the place. I had no idea who was in or out. But I remember thinking when the boys started to settle down about ten that he was in then. I had the impression afterwards that he was in all evening.'

'How was that?'

'There was a faint sound of music at times—I mean, even before ten. That would be when he opened the door. The flat isn't self-contained; they have to use a staff lavatory in the upstairs corridor. At the time I'd not really identified the music. Subconsciously I suppose I'd thought it was a transistor. It was only when I went to the flat that it struck me it could have been his record player I'd heard all evening.'

'What other members of staff were in the building?'

'No one. The kitchen staff leave as soon as supper is served, and the boys wash up, supervised by the duty instructor. It was a Saturday and all the staff were away from the school. My husband went home after tea, and Lithgow lives out too—he's the chief instructor—' She looked uncertain, not knowing the extent of Pryce's knowledge, '—and Paul Wright was off duty.'

91

'Thank you,' he nodded pleasantly, 'you've been very helpful.'

When she had gone, he asked: 'What would Martin's duties be after eleven?'

'If there were no emergencies, nothing,' Ted told him, 'he could go to bed until seven the following morning.'

'What about telephone calls?'

'They would be switched through to his flat. He has two phones: one is his own line, the other's an extension from the small switchboard in the secretary's office.'

'Thank you.' He turned to Miss Pink expansively: 'Now ma'am, can you tell me where the warden was after one-thirty on Sunday afternoon?'

'Only for part of the time; for the rest I believed his own account of his movements.'

'Start from one-thirty.'

'Apparently he was looking for his car until after dark when I met him.' She told him about the meeting on the valley road and the conversation in the Goat. The detective's eyebrows lifted when she came to Martin's reason for not reporting his wife's disappearance: that she might return that night, but he didn't interrupt. She ended with his remark concerning the motive for his search on Sunday afternoon: 'I was looking for my car!'

'That could be taken two ways,' Pryce commented, 'if true it means he thought more of the car than of his wife, but it also means that he didn't know where the car was.'

No one said anything. The sergeant flexed his shoulders and stretched cramped fingers. Pryce looked at Ted.

'You and Miss Pink are watching the interests of the Centre,' he said. It sounded like an accusation.

'Martin is no longer on the strength,' Ted reminded him.

'Yes. This is an odd coincidence: him being dismissed within a few hours of her disappearing. We know she was killed first because this lady with the queer name—Polish, is it? Wolkoff, saw the car about three o'clock on Sunday afternoon but Martin didn't get his marching orders until—' he glanced at Miss Pink, '—after dark anyway.'

'About five-thirty,' she told him.

'So his dismissal could have had nothing to do with her death.' He turned to Ted again. 'You're looking after the Centre's interests,' he repeated.

'We want to see the matter cleared up as soon as possible, naturally. What are Martin's chances?'

'Looks bad for him. How many records can a record player take? Would it play long enough for him to get from here to the coast, dispose of the car and body and drive back?'

'He'd need an accomplice and another car,' Ted pointed out.

'Oh yes, he would that,' Pryce beamed at them generally. Miss Pink felt a twinge of horror which was quickly followed by amusement. Sally as an accomplice? In any event, she thought comfortably, they couldn't both have been away from the building at the same time.

'After eleven,' Pryce said, watching her, and he wasn't smiling now, 'There needn't have been anyone on duty. It was a risk of course, but as long as no boy comes forward to say the duty instructor wasn't in his flat, and no one says they telephoned and couldn't get an answer. . . . We can't prove he wasn't here, but on the other hand he can't prove he was.'

'Do you know what time she was killed?' Miss Pink asked.

'Not to within a few hours, ma'am; stomach contents are unreliable at best and this lady didn't eat much. All we can say is that she'd drunk a lot of whisky, and it's most unlikely she was sober when she died. But so far as the location of the murder's concerned, she could have been killed here and disposed of with the help of an accomplice after the place quietened down.'

'You've got this transport problem,' Ted reminded him, 'She'd left in the Jaguar, and even if she'd come back, where's your second car to bring back the murderer from the coast? It's over eight miles. The chief instructor had the Land Rover, Hughes' car was off the road, and the only other vehicle was a van belonging to Nell Harvey. She was off duty and if she wasn't out in it, I doubt if she'd leave the keys inside.'

Nell was sent for. When she came in she was wearing a short printed dress and she fairly bloomed with health and vitality. Introduced to Pryce she was attentive but a little reserved. Slade and she were out in her van that evening, she said. They returned about eleven-thirty, she had locked the van and taken the keys to her room.

'You didn't happen to see the Jaguar,' Pryce mused, looking at the map, 'which way did you go?'

'We called at one or two places, finishing at the Saracen's Head in Bontddu. We didn't see the car."

'Wrong direction anyway. When you came back, did you see the warden or any indication of his presence: a light in his room for instance?'

'I wouldn't know about that. My room, and Slade's, are in the stable block at the back. The warden's flat faces in a different direction.'

When she'd gone, Pryce turned to Miss Pink.

'Hughes,' he said, 'Rowland Hughes. What's he like, ma'am?'

She said carefully, remembering that Ted had sketched in the staff for him while she was changing: 'He's older than the others, competent, no great initiative—a family man—' She paused. The significance of Hughes at this moment struck her but she didn't continue. However, Pryce knew why she had hesitated.

'If he says his wife came home at eleven would you believe him?'

'Nearer eleven-fifteen at their cottage,' she pointed out. 'It won't make any odds. Hughes is a simple soul and, I imagine, a bad liar. You'll get the truth out of him without any difficulty. You don't seem in any hurry to stop them communicating,' she added obliquely.

'You mean they'll be cooking up a story? They'd have done that Saturday night, ma'am.'

'Look,' Ted said, 'apart from the obstacle of the murderer trying to get back from the coast with no car, surely the only incentive Sally would have to help Martin would be that she

94

was his mistress. Can you see her husband giving her an alibi in those circumstances?'

'It happens the other way round.'

'You mean women giving husbands alibis because they've murdered mistresses. This is rather more involved. What you're suggesting is the husband alibi-ing his wife who's helped murder her lover's wife!'

'Similar thing,' Pryce said phlegmatically, 'let's have him in.'

'I'll go,' Ted said, looking as if he was glad to move.

No one said anything until he returned with Hughes. The man was expressionless.

After some innocuous questions about his position at the Centre, Pryce asked pleasantly:

'How did *you* spend Saturday night?'

Hughes frowned: 'I was off duty,' he said, 'I watched television.'

'What time did you go to bed?'

'About eleven.'

'When did your wife come home?'

'About quarter past.'

'How do you know?'

'I was reading and I didn't like her coming home so late. I was mad, if you want to know.' He was suddenly angry: 'She'd done too much for Martin, always standing in for him, running all the admin. side, and here she's taken over his Saturday evening duty just because he was feeling ill. Ill! He'd got a hangover from the night before and Saturday he just got drunk again. A whole bottle of whisky, she said: empty on the floor when she went in.' He paused.

'What was the weather like?'

'Eh?'

'The weather on Saturday evening?'

'I—What's that got to do with it?'

'Raining?'

'I don't know. I didn't go out.'

'But Mrs Hughes would be wet when she came in, wouldn't she? Her hair would be damp?'

'Not really, she wears one of those plastic hood things when it rains.'

'What time did it start raining?'

'I've no idea, I tell you.'

'Well, we can find that out easily enough. So she wasn't wet when she came in?'

'I can't remember.'

Pryce raised his eyebrows. Hughes shifted uncomfortably. Miss Pink felt frightened. There was something wrong here—or was Hughes like many weak men: always frightened of police questioning? Most people had something to feel guilty about. To her surprise Pryce dismissed the man.

Slade and Wright were left but they were both off duty and not in the building. Miss Pink guessed that they'd deliberately made themselves scarce but she didn't say so. Pryce asked permission to address the boys, when he would suggest that if any of them had information that might be useful they could see him in private.

The directors exchanged glances and nodded. They had little choice. It was stipulated only that the boys should have their supper first and that either Miss Pink or Ted should be present at any subsequent interviews. Pryce agreed. Ted went to find the duty instructor.

'How soon do you expect Martin?' Miss Pink asked.

'I'm waiting for a phone call: to say they've located him. But then it's quite a journey: five or six hours.'

'They'll bring him straight away, without a night's sleep?'

'Oh yes,' he started to fold up the map, 'straight away.' In a different tone he went on: 'There's not much more we can do here after I've spoken to the lads. I'll hang around for a while in case someone's got anything to tell us but I don't set much store by it.'

By nine-thirty Miss Pink was exhausted. Pryce had addressed the boys in the assembly hall but no one had approached him afterwards although the Centre hummed with excitement like a swarm of bees. A call had come through from London to say that Martin was on his way. The directors returned to the Goat feeling flat and dispirited, torn between speculation concerning Martin's guilt, and the suspicion that something was wrong in the Hughes' household. So far as Martin was concerned Miss Pink felt that bewilderment and wretchedness would be as likely felt by a man who'd murdered his wife as by one who'd been cuckolded and deserted, but that in the former case there'd have been horror as well, and this was absent when she talked to Martin on Sunday afternoon. But she was too tired to defend him strenuously and both were too tired to eat more than a little of the soup and cold fowl which Olwen served reproach-fully—for she now knew about the murder, and knew that the others had known when she served their tea.

After supper Miss Pink excused herself and went to her room. She bathed luxuriously, deeply grateful that she hadn't to meet anyone else that night, happy that she'd taken one of the few rooms with a private bathroom so that she didn't now run the risk of meeting Olwen or even Ted in the passage. With the bedside lamp glowing softly in the warm room and the bed turned down, with the latest novel by her current favourites: Sjowall and Wahloo, on the table, she kicked off her slippers—and someone knocked at the door.

She sighed and put on her slippers again.

It was Sally. Miss Pink stared at her, and turned back to find her spectacles.

'I couldn't get away before,' Sally said. She sounded not quite natural. 'It's about the future arrangements.'

Miss Pink invited her in and shut the door.

'Sit down. Won't you have a drink?'

'No, nothing, thank you.'

'Yes.' Miss Pink sat on the edge of the bed since her visitor had the only easy chair. 'Now what's worrying you?'

'How much do we tell the boys?'

'No more than they've been told. It won't hurt them; they didn't really know her. I don't think the horror will get through to them. If it does, I'm afraid it can't be helped.'

97

'And—Martin?'

'Will they know he's here? I suppose they will if the Press see him. I can only suggest you stick to facts and don't speculate. Everyone's innocent until they're proved guilty.' Sally looked at her quickly. 'The best thing, the only thing to do, is to continue as usual: keep to the timetable. Of course there will be a lot of gossip: among the boys, kitchen staff, tradesmen. We have to accept it. And now that's disposed of, tell me what the real trouble is.'

Sally stared at her.

'You didn't come here at this time of night to ask me how the staff should treat the boys; you know as much about adolescents as I do. You're worried about someone—Rowland or Charles?'

There was no beating about the bush.

'I'm afraid Rowland's been rather silly,' Sally admitted, 'you see, it's difficult to describe Bett to anyone who didn't know her, who hadn't seen her with her hair down. She was usually on her best behaviour with the directors—that is, until Saturday. She wasn't very bright but she had an eye to the main chance and she was lazy. Charles was her meal ticket— and security too, of course. So she was careful during directors' weekends and she managed to keep him sober too. I think she frightened him into it. But the rest of the time she didn't even attempt to hide her feelings.'

'Towards whom?'

'Everyone. Men and women. I said she didn't hide her feelings but I don't think she had any besides self-pity. It was odd in a woman of her age. You meet elderly women like this, and their lives revolve round themselves, and everything in life is wrong. Bett was like the Ancient Mariner: she got you in a corner, literally and metaphorically, and poured out her problems. I think she judged people by their capacity as listeners. We all came in for it one time or another.'

'Really,' Miss Pink looked interested, 'but why was she like this? She wasn't unattractive.'

'No—' Sally said doubtfully, 'but she seemed incapable of

having a lasting relationship with anyone. She didn't hit it off with her husband but she didn't with anyone else either. There was no boy friend. I don't think men mattered to her. I think her basic trouble was boredom, and she had this dreadful tendency to carp at everything so that if there was nothing to moan about she invented it.'

'I see,' Miss Pink said untruthfully, 'but where does Rowland come in?'

'Well, he wasn't as wily as the rest of us. He didn't know how to avoid her, and he was sorry for her. He's a bit dim where women are concerned: rather chivalrous and soft—and once she got your attention she became quite subtle: claws inside a velvet glove. So she poured it out and Rowland soaked it up and saw himself as a kind of counsellor, and I think she came to look on him as a father figure. It sounds a bit odd but she was rather retarded and Rowland—well, there wasn't that much difference between her and Jennifer.'

Miss Pink refrained from pointing out that Sally's daughter wasn't retarded and in any case there was a great deal of difference between fifteen and thirty.

'Where did they meet?'

'It only happened once or twice. They went to pubs.'

'Well, that seems quite above-board. I suppose he's worried that someone will come forward who's seen them together?'

'Yes.' She hesitated. Miss Pink saw that there was more to come.

'Did they meet on Saturday evening?' she asked.

'No,' Sally said evenly, 'she wanted him to. But there was a programme on television he wanted to watch. He didn't go.'

'That was sensible, and of course, although you weren't in your house, the children were.'

Sally smiled.

'No, they'd gone into town with a party to the cinema. Rowland was alone.'

'That's not so good.' Miss Pink was feeling a little light-headed. The conversation was like a game: retreat and thrust, retreat. . . .

'It doesn't make any difference,' Sally was saying, 'He rang me at the Centre twice because he was so furious about my not coming home.'

'What time did he ring?'

'Just after supper—about seven-thirty, and again about ten.'

Miss Pink thought: two and a half hours?

'I rang him at nine to remind him to switch the electric blankets on,' Sally said, 'I always do that.'

Chapter Nine

H E S A T H U N C H E D over the table drinking black coffee. He was smoking and his fingers shone with nicotine and sweat. It was warm in the dining room.

Miss Pink, astonished and appalled, stopped beside him.

'Good morning, Charles,' she said quietly.

He took one elbow off the table and leaned back to focus on her. For a moment there was no recognition even as he returned her greeting.

'Please accept my sympathy,' she said, and meant it for, murderer or not, he was obviously in need of compassion.

'Miss Pink.' He announced her name as if he were relaying the information. 'That's kind of you,' he added more naturally.

'Would you like me to sit here?' she asked.

There was a pause.

'Yes,' he said slowly, 'I would.'

She sat down, making a business of it, settled herself and looked out of the window.

'A better morning,' she murmured.

'They let me go,' he said in the same tone in which he would have told her it looked like rain.

'When?'

'I don't know. I've lost count of time but it couldn't have been long ago.'

'Have you had any sleep?'

'No. They said I could sleep today.'

There was another pause.

'How long were you with them?'

'Some time.' He made an attempt to calculate. 'We left London, I suppose about eight last evening. We must have arrived some time after midnight. I've been with them several hours.'

Olwen came in, stared at Miss Pink in consternation and ignored Martin.

'Mr Roberts said to tell you he'd gone with the police, mum.'

Miss Pink would have liked to question her but felt this would be tactless in Martin's presence. She ordered coffee and toast. She could eat only a token breakfast when she was surrounded by tobacco smoke but in the circumstances she hadn't the heart to protest. He lit a fresh cigarette from the stub of the last. There were deep pouches under his eyes and the flesh of his face appeared to have sagged. The suggestion of a tan which he had possessed had faded, leaving his skin an unhealthy yellow.

'Do you want to talk about it?' she asked.

'Not particularly.'

He seemed to be in that state of despondency that takes every word literally and which—sometimes—exposes the truth. But did she want to know the truth? Did she need to? The police had questioned him for several hours and then released him. Was there not enough evidence for a charge or did they think him innocent?

'I want to go there,' he said, 'will you take me?'

'Go where?'

'To the cliffs—where it happened.'

She frowned. 'I'll take you if you're sure you want to go.'

'I haven't a car, you see.'

'You're quite sure you want to go?'

'It's a nagging feeling. I've got nothing to do. They want me to stay here: in the locality. They're not sure of me, I suppose; I'm the obvious person but they don't know how I could have got from the Centre and back without transport. They seem to think Sally's mixed up in it. So I can't go away—and there's the inquest this afternoon, just informal, they say. They said I should get some sleep but I don't think I could sleep. There's nothing I want to do except that on Sunday I looked everywhere and couldn't find her and never caught a glimpse of the car: a blue Jag; you couldn't miss it, could you? Not in this part of the world at this time of year? I want to see it. There must be something. Your eyes will be better than mine.'

She realised he was referring more to her state of mind than her vision. Olwen had come in during this rambling discourse but he didn't notice her. The two women stared at him while the words tipped out as if of their own volition. Olwen put a second pot of coffee and a rack of toast on the table.

'We'll go as soon as I've had my breakfast,' Miss Pink assured him, taking a piece of toast.

When she had finished eating she excused herself and went to the kitchen where she learned that a police car had brought Martin to the Goat shortly before she came down. Ted had been in the hall at that moment. He had gone outside to speak to someone in the car, returned for his coat and to leave the message, then been driven away. The police were staying at a hotel on the main road.

Miss Pink left a message of her own for Ted saying that she had gone to Puffin Cove with Martin.

'Do you think you should?' Olwen asked, eyeing her anxiously.

Miss Pink smiled vaguely and left the kitchen.

Martin lost some of his stiffness on the drive. The cold light of morning emphasised his sunken features cruelly but he was more alive now. He had held the door for her as she got in the Austin and on the way to the coast he glanced at landmarks with occasional interest. When she turned off the main road towards the headland he said with a sudden revelation of feeling:

'Oh, *here?*'

'Didn't they make it plain to you?'

'I don't expect I listened. The place didn't matter then.'

Again she turned left. Martin said wonderingly: 'This is the way to Porth Bach: where we start the canoe expedition.'

As they approached Puffin Cove they saw police cars parked on the verge, the occupants moving purposefully among the gorse. Miss Pink stopped in a passing-place about two hundred yards west of the cars and they continued on foot. Now she could distinguish the solid figure of Pryce, who was talking to his sergeant. The superintendent looked up as they approached and waited. Miss Pink, thinking that perhaps Martin should speak first, glanced at him and saw that he was staring at the marks in the turf below the road. His jaw was clenched and a muscle moved in his cheek. He started down the slope but Pryce moved with surprising speed, taking the other's arm and leading him diagonally towards the cliff and the place from which she had tried to see the Jaguar yesterday.

They stood back a little way from the edge of the cliff but it was Pryce who appeared to be doing the talking. Martin stared downwards with his hands in his pockets. After a while they returned, walking slowly up the line of gouges in the turf. She heard Martin say: 'I wonder if it kept on its wheels; I think it did.'

'Why?' Pryce asked, watching him.

'I used to rally—before I started drinking; I've seen plenty of cars leave the road, and the marks they made.'

He smiled bitterly and Miss Pink thought that he must once have possessed considerable charm: when he was in the Army and there was always someone above to make the big decisions.

'No, it didn't turn over,' he said with more certainty, studying the slope, 'it would have been pointing straight at the sea when it took off, virtually at right angles to the road.'

'Well,' Pryce said genially, 'I've work to do. I'll leave you in this good lady's charge. I'll be sending a car for you this afternoon. The inquest's at three, ma'am; only identification and so on, of course. It'll be adjourned.'

'One of us will be there,' she assured him, 'by the way, where is Mr Roberts?'

'Back at your hotel having breakfast.'

He turned away and crossed the road. Martin suddenly sat down on the turf. 'God, I'm tired,' he sighed.

'I'll take you back and you can get some sleep.'

'I don't feel like going back.'

'Come along,' she said firmly, 'we shall be in the way here.'

'Do *you* think I did it?' he asked as they walked along the road.

'If you did, you're a genius at acting.' There was no necessity to add that she didn't think he could have faked the wretchedness and the shock which he had portrayed throughout right back to Sunday afternoon, particularly that last crazy gesture of claiming he was more interested in his car than his wife. Aloud she said: 'Have you any idea who it could have been?'

'She didn't name him.'

'So you knew there was someone.'

'Oh yes. She told me on Saturday morning. I wasn't ill—at least, it wasn't liver or hangover. I was just—I couldn't face going on the hill with all of you and being polite. I wanted to lie down and go to sleep.'

'Oh dear.'

'Yes, you all thought I was drunk. But the reality was worse. Having lived with my wife for four years I should have built up a resistance to shock. In fact it worked the other way: shock was cumulative. Saturday was the crunch.'

'Have you told the police this?'

'Yes, and the details, except that I don't know much. Only that there was a man and he was going to marry her and she was leaving me next week—that is, this week.'

'She told you this on Saturday morning?'

'At breakfast—what passed for breakfast with us. They—were not pleasant times. I'd pointed out that in a decently run Centre the warden and his wife would have entertained the directors: given them dinner on Saturday night. It developed into a slanging match as any remark could—and did, at the end—and she told me, in detail, what she would be doing that Saturday night.'

His mouth twisted in disgust but it passed and left his face vulnerable. 'Poor kid,' he said with deep feeling. The term puzzled Miss Pink momentarily until she realised that there must be about twenty years difference—had been—between him and his wife.

'But,' she put in, hoping that technical matters might get them away from thoughts that for him must be unbearable: 'As it turned out, it looks as if she was mistaken in thinking he was going to marry her.'

'I expect it was just a taunt.'

'Did you tell the police *that*?'

'I told them the lot. I'm too tired to try to hide anything, and I don't care any longer. All the dirty washing's going to be put on exhibition.'

To her surprise, when they reached the Austin, he insisted on getting in the back where he went to sleep immediately. She didn't enter the car herself but stood watching him through the glass. Eventually she wound down a window to give him air, pocketed the keys and walked back to Pryce.

'A combination of shock and fatigue, don't you think?' she asked, guessing he had watched every move.

He nodded. 'Don't you worry ma'am, we'll keep an eye on him. It's a nice day for a stroll.'

'I'm going to the cove,' Miss Pink said, 'and you?'

'Ah, we're just looking.'

She noticed that they were concentrating on an area of turf and gorse inland of the passing-place. Was that where the Jaguar had been parked? She continued towards Porth Bach wondering how many local men had known Bett Martin, speculating if Pryce had another lead after rejecting Martin, if indeed he had rejected him. He'd been watching the ex-warden very closely on the cliff.

She had not gone far when she was aware of a black figure ahead which she was overtaking. At first she thought it was a policeman, then she saw that the person was wearing a skirt. Where had the woman come from? Certainly it wasn't from the direction of the Schooner Hotel. This must be Mrs Wolkoff. Had she been spying on the police from behind the gorse?

As Miss Pink approached, the woman looked round in

apparent surprise. She wore a black coat and hat, a mauve dress and lace-up shoes with low heels. A pair of field glasses was slung across her flat chest. Her face was beaky with pale eyes behind steel-rimmed spectacles. She moved well but her lined face put her nearer eighty than seventy. She stopped.

'It's a pleasant day for the time of year,' she said, peering at Miss Pink.

'It is. Are you Mrs Wolkoff?'

'You're a tec!' The other beamed in triumph.

'I beg your pardon?'

'A detective,' Mrs Wolkoff repeated uncertainly.

Miss Pink introduced herself but she was listened to with scant attention. She had the impression that the old woman already knew who she was.

'What a terrible time this is for you,' Mrs Wolkoff said with feeling, 'I think you're showing great courage, my dear. Tell me, why isn't he under arrest?' She glanced back along the road.

'Who?'

'Why, the husband, of course.'

'Innocent until proved guilty?' Miss Pink suggested with her vague smile, wondering where else she had heard that recently.

'Oh quite. Quite. British justice is the envy of the world, although even that is not above being rigged on occasion. Back-handers, you know.'

She had a delightful voice, expressive and musical. Every phrase caricatured the feeling it was intended to convey and in those mellifluous tones the curiously dated slang sounded like an obscenity.

'Have you been interviewed by the police?' she asked Miss Pink.

'On occasions.'

'I was referring to our murder.' She waited, her head on one side like a reproachful heron.

'I'm not sure I can help them. Have they been to you?'

Mrs Wolkoff said with gentle reproof: 'I started it all, didn't you know? Perhaps you don't know; they don't seem to have taken you into their confidence. A constable called on Monday evening. He was, I regret to say, round the twist. I had assumed at first that it was merely another case of disposing of an unwanted car but his training should have made him suspicious. The tec was a different calibre altogether: very polite and appreciative.'

'Superintendent Pryce?'

'Is that his name? It had slipped my memory. Yes, he called on me this morning.'

She stopped as if waiting for a cue so Miss Pink asked if the police had been interested in the events of Saturday night. A look of cunning appeared on Mrs Wolkoff's face. Miss Pink guessed that she was enjoying herself but she realised, not without surprise, that morbid curiosity didn't appear to be at the bottom of the enjoyment.

'Saturday night is what they're interested in, of course,' she agreed, 'but they've drawn a blank. I don't go out after dark.'

'Not at all?'

'No. No one in their right senses would walk this path after dark.'

'What are you afraid of? And if it's there in the dark, where is it in the daytime?'

'It's not a joking matter,' she reproved sharply, 'the track's dangerous, lethal. Look at it! If you strayed off the tar macadam in the dark, there's nothing to stop you tumbling in the drink. I'm out a lot in the daytime; I watch birds, d'you see. But in the evenings I look at television or I work. I'm a very busy woman.'

As they walked along the road Miss Pink learned that her companion had married a White Russian in Paris during the twenties. He was, according to his widow, a charming and cultured nobleman who possessed a few family jewels salvaged from the revolution, but no business sense. His projects lost money, he went bankrupt—and sold another gem to finance the next enterprise. They had lived in the United States, Morocco, Istanbul, Rio de Janeiro. There were no children. Mrs Wolkoff didn't elaborate on her husband's projects. Miss Pink was sorry and wondered if they were too colourful for even his widow to do justice to them.

From the top of the hill where the road started to descend she looked at Porth Bach with fresh interest.

'How lonely is it?' she asked, aware that even in this context appearances might be deceptive, as her companion confirmed.

'There is your own organisation,' she pointed out, twinkling girlishly at the other, 'I know them all—all the instructors, that is,' she corrected herself quickly, not wanting her listener to think she associated with people like the Martins, 'and then almost every weekend there are the skin divers—'

'Have you a sunken ship here?'

The woman looked arch and put a finger to her lips.

'My dear, underwater exploration is cloak and dagger stuff. Another club might steal a march on you. It's the same in the world of climbing and first ascents.'

Mis Pink was startled. Mrs Wolkoff might be eccentric but she was unusually well-informed.

'Your house is rather isolated at the top of the cove,' she observed, and was intrigued to catch a sharp glance from the other.

'Yes, we're fortunate in that respect. The trees hide us from each other. None of us knows what's going on in the other houses.'

'Are they pleasant neighbours, when the houses are occupied?'

'Very pleasant, on the whole. You understand that in the high season there is a constant coming and going: short lets, you know. Usually I see the owners of the properties in spring and autumn only although some run down during the season to see that the cottages have been left in good condition for the next visitors, or carry out some repairs.'

'I suppose you keep an eye on the places when they're empty.'

'Certainly not. I am not a caretaker.'

Miss Pink made no rejoinder. They had reached the elbow and now the old woman left the road and led the way down a path to the stream which they crossed by planks with an iron handrail. The path ended at the gate of her cottage. The garden was wild even for late autumn and there was no sign of cultivation other than two or three straggling bushes of Michaelmas daisies.

The key was produced (it was round her hostess's neck on a piece of black tape) and Miss Pink was ushered into a dark interior that smelt of dead ashes and damp. The light was switched on and she saw a living room so cluttered with old furniture that any progress between the pieces had to be in the nature of a sidle. On every flat surface there were books and files, journals, newspapers, and letter racks crammed with papers. Two huge hardboard panels hung on one wall, trellissed with tape: the kind used in country hotels for residents' mail. These were covered with what Miss Pink took to be letters.

There was an old and dirty range with an iron kettle on a gantry, and the mantelshelf was covered with a brown velvet cloth fringed with bobbles. There were two good china King Charles spaniels on the shelf. A television set was on an occasional table by the range. A tall filing cabinet and a smaller one for card indices stood against one wall.

On the large round mahogany table which took up all the centre of the room Mrs Wolkoff was working on a project. An ancient standard typewriter was surrounded by tracing and drawing paper, maps, files, coloured pencils.

Miss Pink was looking at the books when her hostess came in from the kitchen with cups of coffee.

'I'm afraid it's only powder.' She glanced at the book in her guest's hands. 'Have you read the Protocols?'

'Yes.' Miss Pink returned the book to its shelf.

'And what did you think of it?'

'Horrifying.'

'Yes. And it's all coming true. The Zionists have infiltrated every profession: politics, industry, finance, particularly finance.'

'Short-term profits,' Miss Pink murmured.

'Exactly: a world-wide conspiracy for world government. Society is riddled. The Enemy is within the gate. But a few people are aware of what is happening, and we disseminate information. It isn't all that difficult to uncover the evidence, given a good agent and the knowledge that it's there.'

'Evidence?'

'We hear a great deal by way of leaks, you know, from behind closed doors. The devil hasn't all the best tunes.' She chuckled. 'D'you know what I mean by that?'

'No.'

'Bugging! Line tapping! Telephoto lenses! *We* infiltrate too But it's dangerous work. There's no hope for anyone if he's caught. No praise if they succeed, disowned if they fail.'

'Where do you recruit them?'

'That I can't tell you. I don't really know myself. I can guess. I have a shrewd idea but, no, you shouldn't ask.'

'I'm sorry. But your work here can't be secret; you've shown it to me—that is, I can see it.'

As she said this Miss Pink was acutely aware of her vulnerability: no other person nearer than the cliff top—or was there? No telephone. But there was a telephone somewhere: Mrs Wolkoff had used it to contact the public health inspector. Was it upstairs or had she gone to the hotel?

She was saying: '*My* work isn't secret. I'm going to publish it.' She gestured at a row of box files on a massive sideboard. 'Those are my dossiers.'

'Yes?'

'I compile dossiers on all those in the conspiracy or in any way related to it, knowingly or unwittingly. And all this information is available to the police or Interpol at any time they may need it. We have names and addresses and even ex-directory telephone numbers. We know, to a great extent, the exact movements at any given time of all those in the plot.'

Miss Pink felt the hair move on the back of her neck.

'You do all this?'

'Oh, no, indeed. There are numbers of us at work all over the country and in the Commonwealth. We exchange information. Nothing escapes us. . . .'

Miss Pink sat and sipped her coffee, listening to the sound

III

of the beautiful voice, wondering if anything would be said which had a bearing on her own interests, wondering if anyone she knew merited a dossier. She hoped not.

When the time came to go, Mrs Wolkoff insisted on accompanying her guest to her car. Miss Pink protested but, realising that the old lady was determined to have another look at the police, she didn't argue and they set off together.

On the other side of the bridge Miss Pink looked back at the cottage and asked with just the right degree of interest what species of bird were in the area. She noted that telephone wires entered the house from a pole on the inland side.

'A pair of buzzards,' Mrs Wolkoff said with enthusiasm, 'Pied flycatchers, common redstarts; it's possible—'

A jay screamed and came streaking towards them from the wooded slope behind the cottage. The old woman stopped talking so suddenly that Miss Pink turned and saw another kind of excitement replace the enthusiasm for birds.

'Someone about,' Miss Pink said.

Mrs Wolkoff turned her wide gaze on her visitor.

'There's a wild cat in the woods,' she said.

'Really.' Miss Pink stared hard at the slope behind the cottage.

'Come along,' Mrs Wolkoff urged, 'I'm keeping you from your duties.' She touched the other's elbow and chivvied her up the path.

They returned to the cliffs with the younger woman still trying to lure her hostess away from the dangers of world government. In this she was unsuccessful until they came in sight of the now familiar passing-place and before she had time to notice anything out of the ordinary, Mrs Wolkoff remarked:

'And now what's the game?'

Miss Pink followed the direction of her glance.

'I don't see anyone,' she said, 'and the cars have gone.'

'Quite. Do you know why they were here?'

'I assume the Jaguar was parked here.'

'But it wasn't,' Mrs Wolkoff said in the tone of a child being superior: 'It was at the next lay-by.'

'So you were here.' Miss Pink smiled at her.

The old woman smiled back roguishly and wagged her finger.

'Oh no, indeed I wasn't, but I've got a head on my shoulders, and I've had nearly three days to find out where that car was parked. I didn't tell the tec though. We must keep them on their toes, musn't we?'

'How did you find out?'

'Tracks. There's the mark of a tyre on the cliff path; the same tyre has made marks behind the gorse at the next lay-by. I see someone's cottoned on to it; there's a car here.'

'That's my car,' Miss Pink said.

'Indeed? And who is in it?'

'Charles Martin.'

The old woman looked at her without expression, then her face became animated again. 'Come here,' she ordered, 'I'll show you the tyre mark.'

With amazing agility she trotted down the steep grass to the imprint which Miss Pink had noticed the day before. Miss Pink studied the pattern, nodded, and they climbed the bank again and walked to the car. Martin was still asleep.

Behind the gorse Mrs Wolkoff moved over the turf in little rushes like a hen looking for corn. There was quite a lot of litter: cigarette stubs, scraps of paper. Something cleaner, lighter than the rest showed in a patch of sandy earth. Miss Pink stooped to pick it up. It was metal and was embedded in the ground. She prised it out without difficulty. It was a cigarette lighter.

Mrs Wolkoff came and peered at it then at Miss Pink.

'Now how did I come to miss that?' she asked, 'you must take it to the police. Here is that tyre mark, come and look.'

Miss Pink stared at the print and saw that it was similar to the other on the cliff path. No doubt the police would compare moulds or photographs. She assured the old lady that she would tell them about it and, ascertaining that she couldn't give the other a lift (thus confirming her belief that the second excursion to the cliff had the same purpose as the first: curiosity), she said goodbye.

She watched Martin carefully as she slipped the lighter under some maps on the parcel shelf but his eyes didn't open. It was only when she sat on the driver's seat, rocking the car, that he woke. She didn't allow him time to recover his senses before telling him to sit in the front. Mrs Wolkoff watched these proceedings with intense interest but as Miss Pink turned and drove away, the old lady gave a wave that was almost absent-minded and in the mirror Miss Pink saw her start to walk quickly back towards Porth Bach.

A police car was parked at the junction where the road went off to the headland and the Schooner. She didn't stop. Martin took a packet of cigarettes from his pocket and extracted one.

'Lighter under the maps,' she said, pointing.

He leaned forward and picked it out, checked, offered her a cigarette which she declined, and fumbled with the lighter. She drove slowly, watching his hands. After a moment he lit it, and his cigarette, and drew smoke deep into his lungs. He replaced the lighter, stretched his legs as far as was possible and said with the ghost of a chuckle: 'I see you were trapped by Mrs Wolkoff. . . .'

Chapter Ten

THE TABLE TOP was pale green and spotless. Mudstains on the lighter made it look incongruous lying on the formica and, if you knew where it had been found, even a little sinister.

Hughes laughed.

'Well, thanks,' he said, 'where did you find it?'

'It is yours?'

'Oh yes, it's mine. Didn't you know?'

'No, I didn't know.'

The amusement left his face and he became wary.

'Where did you find it?' he repeated.

She told him.

They had been standing in the kitchen of the Hughes' cottage. She had dropped Martin at the Goat where she learned that Ted had telephoned to say he was at the Centre. On arrival at Plas Mawr she was told that Sally, the police and Ted were in the warden's office and not to be disturbed, and that Rowland Hughes had gone home to get some climbing equipment. Miss Pink found him alone.

He sat down in a chair. He was still staring at the lighter but he didn't touch it. There was no expression on his face. After a while she sat down opposite him At least two minutes elapsed before she said:

'It will have to go to the police.'

Still he didn't speak.

'It might look better if you took it,' she said.

He shook his head.

'I didn't kill her.'

'You were there.'

'No! Sally knows!' He looked round wildly and heaved himself to his feet. 'Where is she? Still with the police?

I've got an alibi, you can't shake that. Who do you think you are anyway? Come here raking up the mud, interfering with people's private lives; what business is it of yours? My marriage is sacrosanct. . . .' He stopped, breathing hard, staring at her. He had forgotten what he was saying. 'You've got no right to badger . . . keep nagging at a chap . . . If we're in-efficient, O.K. we get the sack—' his face cleared, 'but not for anything else; I'm telling you here and now—' his red face glowered at her as he leaned across the table, 'our lives are our own outside working hours. No one ever complained before. It's no good you sitting there sneering; you don't know what I'm talking about. I tell you I'm happily married!'

He shouted this and brought his fist down on the table so that the lighter jumped in the air. He snatched it up, eyeing her belligerently, as if daring her to stop him.

The door opened and Sally came in quickly. He made to swing round but her hand was on his shoulder, holding him down, kneading the tweed of his jacket. Her eyes were terrified and she was breathing hard as if she had run all the way from the school.

'Miss Pink will think you're drunk, darling,' she said, enunciating with difficulty. She waited a moment but he said nothing. Carefully, as if ready at a sign to return to him, she came round the table so that she could look at him without Miss Pink seeing her face. The older woman watched Hughes watching his wife.

'Sit down, Sally,' Miss Pink said firmly, 'I found Rowland's lighter where the Jaguar was parked on the cliff top.'

Sally went so white that the older woman moved to catch her but the girl sat down slowly, staring at the man. He looked contrite.

'I'm sorry,' he muttered, and reached to take her hand.

Sally said hopelessly to Miss Pink: 'What are you going to do?'

'It will have to go to the police.'

'No one will believe me,' he said.

'They can't prove anything, darling.'

'What?' he glared at her.

'I said—'

'I heard you: "they can't prove anything"! You think I did it!'

She threw an anguished glance at Miss Pink, willing her to leave. Hughes dropped on his knees and gripped his wife's elbows.

'*You* think I did it!' he repeated, 'but you believed me on Sunday.'

'I still believe you.' She sounded exhausted. 'Don't worry; you didn't do it.' She turned to Miss Pink. 'Why should he do it? I knew, and we all guessed, that the Martins would be dismissed. In fact, I would have tipped you off if you hadn't decided yourselves to sack him. So why on earth should it be Rowland? He had no motive.'

She pushed her husband back. He got up and sat on his chair again, put his elbows on the table and his head in his hands. Sally got up and filled a kettle at the sink. She sighed heavily. The sound was loud in the quiet room. Hughes threw her a resentful glance and fumbled in his pocket for cigarettes. He pulled out the lighter and stared at it, frowning.

'Who told you it was mine?' His tone was full of hostility.

'You're the only one who smokes.'

'There's Martin,' he said quickly.

There was silence as Sally stopped clattering cups in saucers.

'What was she doing last time you saw her?' Miss Pink asked.

'Who?'

'Bett.'

'She was laughing,' he said sullenly.

'At what?'

'Me feeling ill. Whisky always makes me ill.'

'How much did you drink?'

'I don't know. We were drinking from the bottle.'

'Tell me what happened when you were ill.'

He glared at her. Sally said with thinly disguised urgency: 'Tell her, darling.'

He looked at her doubtfully.

'How can I tell what I'm not sure of? You saw me sober but I'd walked it off by the time I got back: eight miles in the rain. I wasn't just drunk on the cliff, I was ill too. It's like a nightmare. I thought it was. I told you.'

'Tell Miss Pink what you told me.'

'It's nothing much. The air hit me as I got out of the car. We'd been running the engine for the heater and the air seemed like a refrigerator: took my breath away, more like an anaesthetic really. I started to walk away and must have gone some distance when I fell over. It seemed to take a long time— falling. Then I went to sleep, or passed out. I don't remember anything until I woke up feeling very cold, and soaked to the skin. It never stopped raining that night. I know. I was out in it most of the time.'

'What did you do when you woke up?' Miss Pink prompted him.

'I went back to the Jag of course, and it wasn't there.'

He stopped. He needed a lot of encouragement.

'Did you look for it?'

'Why should I? I thought she'd gone home and when I looked at my watch it was eleven o'clock so I'd passed out for about two hours or something like that, so I just thought she'd got tired of waiting and gone.'

'Leaving you to walk?'

'She did things like that. Besides she was drunk. I couldn't have done anything even if I'd *known*. There was no sign— whoever had been there was well away, so she was dead long before I came round. She must have been.'

His eyes pleaded frantically. The kettle boiled and Sally switched it off, then stayed motionless. Miss Pink, who considered a guilty conscience was his just desert, asked coldly: 'How did you get home?'

'Walked.'

'What time did you get in?'

'About two, wasn't it?' He looked at Sally. She nodded.

'Could she drive the Jaguar?' Miss Pink asked.

He hesitated. 'More or less.'

'Did she drive to the coast, or you?'

It was too late for blustering but habit died hard and he was visibly restraining himself.

'I drove,' he said. Then with a poor travesty of his old manner: 'Only one thing worse than a woman driver: a woman learner driver!' He checked, inhaling through his nose.

'Where did she meet you?'

'At the bottom of the drive.'

Miss Pink stood up and Sally faced her. The younger woman said accusingly:

'You won't ask any more questions because you want to spare me but I know what you're thinking: that, giving him the benefit of the doubt, she died more or less naturally—a combination of drugs and alcohol perhaps—and when he got back to the car she was dead. So he panicked and pushed the car over the edge.'

Miss Pink watched her carefully.

'You think that's what happened, don't you?' Sally urged, her eyes searching the other's face.

'No.'

'Why not?'

Miss Pink sighed and walked out of the cottage to her car. Sally turned to her husband.

'Why couldn't it have happened like that: dying naturally from an overdose of drugs and alcohol? Lots of people must have got away with it by saying they panicked and hid the body because they thought they wouldn't be believed.'

He looked at her with dull eyes. 'She was strangled,' he said, 'remember?'

The superintendent made no attempt to hide his disapproval.

'With something as important as this you should have brought it to us straight away, ma'am,' he said heavily, turning the lighter in his gloved hand, 'and what with your prints, and Hughes', and Martin's, it's hardly worth the gesture of sending it to the lab.'

She pointed out that he'd left strict instructions not to be disturbed. He grunted and went out to his car followed by the sergeant.

'Hughes.' Ted said reflectively, as they stood at the entrance to Plas Mawr watching the retreating car. 'Pryce is jumping about a bit. It was Sally just now. He maintains, and he may be right, that it's the quiet efficient women who make the best murderers—or the worst, depending how you look at it.'

She glanced at him uneasily and then behind him to the hall. By tacit agreement they started to stroll in the grounds.

'Begin at the beginning,' she ordered, once she was sure they couldn't be overheard, 'when you went away with the police early this morning. What was the purpose of that?'

'I think Pryce was flummoxed and he wanted to pick my brains for more information on the staff and wives. There isn't enough evidence to charge Martin. In fact, there's none. There's an over-riding motive though. Bett was having an affair—' Seeing her expression he stopped.

'He told me.'

'Yes. Well, they can't shake his story; he was drunk when he was picked up in London and he slept during most of the journey. He wasn't fresh when he arrived here and he was exhausted when they finished with him. But his account never varied and it's the same in substance as what he told you Sunday afternoon. On the other hand, if he did do it, he had to have an accomplice because of the transport problem. Pryce let him go but I expect he's being watched, on the assumption that if someone helped, Martin will try to contact him—or her.'

'But, Sally,' Miss Pink exclaimed. 'What made him think of her—as a murderer?'

'Presumably a natural progression from thinking of her as an accomplice. If she wasn't the latter because there was no evidence against Martin, could she be the former? I pointed out that he didn't know her character and he retorted: "Are you sure you do?" which gave me an unpleasant feeling. I'd have taken my oath on her integrity.'

'Exactly—but when it comes to a conflict of loyalties the

family wins. With hindsight, what she did was in character. She'd tell lies to give her husband a false alibi but it's out of the question that she would help Martin murder his wife. I knew she was protecting Hughes when she came to the Goat last night, but I didn't know to what extent she needed to protect him.' She told him about Sally's visit to her room. 'Sally thinks Hughes killed Bett,' she ended simply.

'Do you?'

'He's consumed by guilt but whether that's inspired by deceit or murder is another matter. He's a weak, shallow man, but shrewd. He would probably think he was playing the girl along when in reality it was the reverse. By the time he realised he was embroiled, it was too late.'

'Embroiled? Oh, come!' Ted reproved gently.

'No, no. His distaste for her didn't start with his terror of being suspected of her death, I'm certain of that. He would never jeopardize his marriage—you know the type: that plays around but never gets seriously involved with other women if it can possibly be helped. But Hughes isn't clever enough for that game. I think Bett had a hold over him.'

'Blackmail?'

'Emotional blackmail, yes. She was bored to death, as much with the Centre's atmosphere, I should think, as with her husband. Hughes is lazy and feckless but he was something to tide her over the gap until she could find a man who would look after her better. I don't think there's any doubt that he was the man she told Martin was going to marry her.'

'How would she get him to leave Sally?'

'Possibly by telling him she was pregnant—no, that's too obvious—'

'Women still get murdered for it, but they're silly women: the kind that's murder-prone. It's a hell of a risk for a woman to run, with some men. And she *laughed* at him!'

'No,' Miss Pink said, 'there's something that doesn't fit. The characters are right and the situation would be in character for both of them, but there's something wrong. It's not his lighter:

he could have faked his surpise over my finding it; there's something wrong with the *times*. By the way, how did Pryce get to the cliff before me this morning when they hadn't brought you back before I left the Goat? Is there another way down to Porth Bach?'

'Across the fields? There could be. But Pryce went straight to the cove from his hotel which must have been while you were having breakfast, and I walked back.'

'But then when did he see Mrs Wolkoff?'

'Very early. He left Williams questioning Martin at one time.'

'Well, well.' She told him about the cottage full of dossiers. 'Perhaps,' she said smiling, 'the police have got her on their list of militant revolutionaries.'

Ted gave a bark of laughter. 'I didn't tell you they'd found one of the missing lorries. Could Mrs Wolkoff have been the driver, d'you think?'

She smiled absently. 'Where?'

'In the bottom of a wooded ravine near Clapham, in Yorkshire.'

'A lot of caves near there.'

'Exactly.'

'Did they think the lorry was being driven to one and went off the road?'

'Either that or it was returning. There was nothing in it.'

'It *was* one of the stolen lorries?'

'Oh yes. They'd changed the flashes but it was one of the batch stolen from the Midlands last Friday. Incidentally, no other Service vehicles have been reported missing.'

They were silent for a moment then Miss Pink asked: 'Why would they want to stockpile explosives in this country? I like that even less than shipping them out. I suppose that's selfishness.'

'It's more sinister,' he agreed, 'we've got used to violence in Ireland, but we did think it was contained there.'

Inside the building the bell went for the afternoon session and they glanced at each other guiltily. The routine work of the

Centre continued in the face of increasingly difficult conditions. It was Nell's day off, there was no warden, and neither of the directors ventured an opinion as to when or if Hughes would return. There was no sign of him, nor of Sally. Fortunately the Centre was engaged on indoor activities this Wednesday afternoon, for on the two following days they had the mountaineering expedition which ended the course. Nevertheless, Miss Pink and Ted would have gladly offered their services but for the fact that the inquest was at three. In the end they compromised and while Miss Pink stayed at the Centre to see if she could make anything of the office work, Ted left to attend the inquest.

After three hours, at the end of which she felt she had done little more than make a gesture but exhausted herself in the process, she left Plas Mawr and drove to the Goat where she was suddenly, and to her great surprise—for she had forgotten their existence—accosted by the Press in the person of a stout and middle-aged Peter Pan with sideboards and a bow tie. She gave him the agreed statement and then became so vague as to appear quite silly but for all that, and in addition to reminding the man that Martin wasn't employed by the Centre, she allowed two facts to emerge: the name of the detectives' hotel and the point that the inquest was over. The man was seasoned and knew that the latter had no interest, but then neither had Miss Pink, and he left to find the police.

'They'd run the superintendent to earth soon enough, anyway,' she told the lurking Olwen as the front door closed, 'and it gets them off our backs for the time being.'

'Will I tell them all where the poliss is staying?'

'Yes, you do that. Is there nothing else you can tell them to stop them coming here?'

'We can't have them, mum, not to stay. There's no one for behind the bar after half past ten. We shan't get many asking, anyway. There's a flock of them at Bontddu, all waiting for one of them lorries to go off the road with a load of bombs.'

Ted came upstairs soon after Miss Pink. The inquest had been adjourned and there were no new developments. They went down together and as they came into the hall, Sally got up from a corner and come towards them. Miss Pink was touched by her obvious distress. If murder wasn't the worst crime, she thought, taking the girl's hands and drawing her to the fire, it certainly had cruel effects on the widest circle.

'They've taken him away,' Sally said.

'Not arrested?'

'I don't think so. They said they wanted him for questioning. He agreed to go. I think he wanted to. He was thinking of the children coming home, you see.'

'Good,' Miss Pink said absently, meaning good that he hadn't been arrested—yet, 'now tell me—damn! Have you had tea?'

'It's coming,' Ted said, approaching from the kitchen. Miss Pink realised he must have gone straight there on seeing Sally's face. He was carrying a glass of brandy which he put in front of her.

'Thanks,' Sally whispered and drank some. She put down the glass and said dully: 'I lied to you all the way through.'

'Think nothing of it,' Miss Pink said cheerfully, 'anyone would have done the same.'

Sally stared but the older woman's eyes didn't waver behind the thick lenses. Olwen came in with a large tea-tray.

'Had it ready tonight, mum,' she explained in triumph, working between the furniture like an athlete in an obstacle race. 'You'll be needing it, all of you.' She glanced at the hearth: 'Got plenty of woods there. There's your tea then, and there's something to do with a cock for dinner. He'll need a lot of stewing, I said: an old cock, why didn't you get a nice young chicken, I said, from Ellis Free Range, all running about in the muck and no chemicals, but I suppose she knows what she's doing. It come from Ellis anyway.'

'Woods?' Sally asked when Olwen had gone.

'Logs,' Miss Pink explained, 'and the cock will be *coq au vin*. You'll stay and have dinner with us?'

'No, I must get back to the children. I came to apologise and to tell you—' She frowned and passed a hand over her eyes. Miss Pink poured tea imperturbably.

'It's gone,' Sally said, 'it'll come back. Something Rowland told me to tell you.'

They drank tea and munched scones and Miss Pink thought how cosy their little group would look to a stranger coming in the door.

'He's not wicked.' Sally's words dropped into the silence.

'Oh no,' Ted sounded shocked, 'not *wicked*.'

'It all happened so logically,' she went on, 'when you look back on it, events seemed to march like Fate. I feel like a puppet and, God knows, thinking of them, Bett and Rowland and Charles—oh, definitely puppets.'

Miss Pink studied her thoughtfully. Ted continued to eat, listening and watching.

'Some of what I told you was the truth,' Sally continued, 'quite a lot. I just twisted the facts.'

'I know,' Miss Pink said, rousing herself.

'You mean, you knew I was lying?'

'I know now—although even at the time your attitudes varied, and widely. One day you implied Bett was a nympho-maniac, the next you went out of your way to persuade me that she was a kind of asexual nuisance. I see why—now.'

'She was promiscuous though, and she was a moaner but yes, I did try to change the emphasis. The truth is that she was both and she *clung*: you couldn't get rid of her—'

She stopped, horrified.

'There's no point in not saying it,' Miss Pink said equably, 'you're not giving anything away.'

'What can I do?'

Ted said kindly: 'He's not charged yet.' As if reminded of something he added: 'I ought to telephone,' and went away.

'How long have you known about Bett and Rowland?' Miss Pink asked.

'I'd guessed all along but I couldn't do anything. I just had to stand by and watch him growing more guilty and frightened and then when he did tell me it was too late to do anything. It had been done, *but not by Rowland*!'

'Why did he go up on the cliffs with her?'

125

Sally shrugged miserably. She was still fighting.

'Was she trying to persuade him to go away with her?'

'How did you know?'

'But why didn't he just tell her to—' she had nearly said "go and jump in the sea".

'He was frightened of her. That's probably why he drank the whisky. He knew he'd be terribly ill. It was a kind of defence mechanism: to get away from her. But she was alive when he left her. There was no need at all to tell me where he'd been when he got in on Sunday morning, but he did.'

'There was a need. He had to have your alibi.'

Sally sank back in the depths of her chair. She stared at the fire and suddenly her eyes widened and she sat up, gazing at Miss Pink with a kind of awe.

'No,' she said, 'you're wrong! He didn't tell me because of that. We planned that much later: the following evening, after you'd phoned to say the car had been found. He couldn't have done it. Don't you see? When he came home early Sunday morning all he told me was that he'd been on the cliff top and she'd left him to walk home. Suppose he *had* killed her: he didn't know how soon the car would be found. It could have been seen Sunday morning. But he didn't ask me to work out an alibi until Monday evening!'

'That's it,' Miss Pink said, herself looking quite pleased. 'I thought there was something wrong with the planning if Rowland had done it. Of course, you would have talked to me about him (and, incidentally, established his alibi) on Sunday or Monday, not waited till the car was found. But why did you plan an alibi Monday evening? We didn't know she was in the car till Tuesday.'

'Everyone suspected it,' Sally said impatiently. 'The alibi was only to be used if it was necessary. I'm quite certain he didn't know she'd been murdered, though. *That* threw him and then, on Tuesday evening when the police appeared to suspect me, and asked him questions about me coming in, and about the rain, he nearly broke down. We'd arranged a story to protect *him* but he couldn't think quickly enough to know if the lies in that story might involve me. They were asking the wrong questions.'

Miss Pink nodded agreement. 'The police are going to be awkward,' she said.

'It doesn't matter. I know he didn't do it. He knows. Everything will be all right. The trouble was, I really did think he'd done it; a kind of accident perhaps, putting his hands on her throat to stop her laughing, and pressing too hard. You look worried, Miss Pink. You believe me, don't you?'

'Yes, my dear, but if Rowland's in the clear, who did it?'

Chapter Eleven

'IT WOULD BE pretty conclusive if it were true,' Ted commented.

She'd found him in his room where he had gone when it occurred to him that Sally would talk more freely to Miss Pink on her own.

'I believe her,' she said flatly, 'it was obvious that she couldn't believe it herself when she realised the significance of Rowland not troubling about an alibi for so long after Bett died. Suddenly she stopped being desperate and there was a complete reversal of feeling. She can't fabricate facial expressions and she can't hide them, otherwise she wouldn't have looked so stricken when Llewelyn rang yesterday afternoon. She guessed then what the results of the post mortem were. She'd dreaded it from the moment she heard the car hadn't left the area but was in the sea. Hughes had assured her that Bett was alive when he left her, but the poor chap can't even tell the truth convincingly.'

Ted thought about this for a moment, then he said: 'If we work from the premise that Sally is telling the truth now, then there was a third person on the cliff. Hughes could be keeping quiet about him.'

'No. He's a very frightened man, and if he'd known that a third person was present, he'd be the first to say so. And if he's innocent of the murder he can't have been an accomplice; in fact when I saw him this morning, it was only in passing that he mentioned a third person, and that's a big point in his favour because if he'd been guilty he'd have had a suspect all lined up for us. He did make a clumsy attempt to implicate Martin but that was spontaneous.'

'Yes, he's too stupid to be a murderer. But it's odd about

that lighter. Your widow woman sounds as if she wouldn't have missed it when she was looking for the tyre marks. It was very likely planted. I wonder when he lost it. No, the question is: when was he last seen with it in his possession?'

Miss Pink telephoned Sally: 'About Rowland's lighter: do you know when he lost it?'

'But that's what I meant to tell you: why I came to the Goat! He told me to tell you he had it Sunday, possibly even on Monday.'

'When on Sunday?'

'In the afternoon. He remembered using it at the Centre. He came down after lunch and spent the afternoon reading the papers.'

'It wouldn't stand up in court,' Ted said when she returned to him, 'what's needed is an impartial witness who saw him with it after Saturday night. She will have realised that by now too. I wouldn't be surprised if, within the next few hours, some-one rings up to tell us he, or she, saw Rowland lighting a cigarette on Sunday.'

She nodded and frowned at the empty lounge. 'Where's Martin?' she asked, 'I haven't seen him since lunch time.'

'I expect he's asleep.' Ted was casual.

Miss Pink said: 'Do you remember how puzzled we were to think why Bett Martin went down to the cliffs?'

'So?'

'Now we know. But what kind of thing would take a *third* party down there?'

'It probably has as logical an explanation as the one for Bett's visit. What about Mrs Wolkoff?'

She opened her mouth to protest and stopped. They were both silent for some time.

'I haven't met her,' Ted pointed out.

'You should. We'll go there tomorrow. I wonder if she can drive. What motive could she have?'

'Would she need a reasonable one?'

'Well, there are degrees of madness but the more I think

129

about her the wider the gap becomes between her particular lack of balance and homicidal mania. She could do a lot of harm by talk and letters (signed, I think, not anonymous) but I can't associate her with physical violence. She's stupid and stubborn and dangerous but she's not ruthless.'

'Do you think she has visitors: people mixed up with this anti-Semitism business?'

'That's a point, but how could she or her visitor have got hold of Rowland's lighter? It comes back to the Centre. Who came along that road between nine and eleven o'clock and why? Dawson of the Schooner might very well be visiting Mrs Wolkoff, if they're friendly, but no: as the Americans say, we're reaching.'

'So if we say it was someone at the Centre and we rule out Martin and Hughes, we're left with Slade, Paul Wright and Lithgow.'

'Slade and Nell were—' She stopped as Olwen came in and, with a pointed look at Miss Pink's breeches asked if they would like to order the wine. Thus reminded of the time, they went upstairs, bathed and changed hurriedly but were further delayed from resuming their conversation by the presence of Olwen while they ate their *moules marinières* and subsequently by the delights of the *coq au vin*. They were silent until the Stilton had come and been regretfully refused and then it was Olwen who broke the silence:

'There's one of your people outside, wants to see you.'

'Which one?' Ted asked.

'The nice one with curly hair, reddish it is.'

'Paul,' Miss Pink said. She looked at Ted who nodded. 'Ask him to come in, and bring another cup.'

He came in apologising profusely. He hadn't meant to interrupt; he would wait till they'd finished. Ted told him to draw up a chair and Olwen brought coffee. Asked what he would drink, Paul's eyes went to Ted's brandy glass. Miss Pink excused herself and went to the kitchen. Olwen and Miss Devereux, a blue-haired lady with a generous bosom and fine legs, were sitting at the scrubbed table enjoying the last of the chicken. Miss Pink complimented the chef and asked Olwen to take the Martell and leave it on the table. Miss Devereux sat back in her chair and regarded the visitor shrewdly.

'He didn't do it,' she said.

'I'm inclined to agree, but why do you think so?'

'Boys like him don't kill women like her. And he was in the bar from about nine till ten-thirty, then he had to walk home. The barman will swear to it. Leaves you with the boxer type and the wee Scot,' she ended coolly. 'Take your pick.'

'Which do you favour?' Miss Pink asked, fully aware that, in the absence of Olwen, there was no witnesses to this conversation.

Miss Devereux selected a toothpick from a Bernard Leach bowl and regarded it thoughtfully.

'Nothing to choose between 'em,' she said.

'They're still questioning Rowland,' Ted told her as a kind of introduction when she returned.

'The reporters came up and told us,' Paul informed her eagerly. 'We had no comment to make. But I wanted to see you about Rowland. You were asking Sally when he lost his lighter. I can't tell you when he *lost* it but he had it Monday morning at breakfast. I remember because I hate people who smoke at the table and I always try to finish before him but he didn't have bacon Monday, seemed off his feed—and no wonder, seeing the mess he'd got himself into—so he lit up before I'd finished and I remember that click of his lighter: a terribly meaningful sound, then a cloud of smoke all over the table.'

'He definitely used the lighter, not a match?'

'Oh, definitely. It's a different action, isn't it? Two hands for matches, only one for a lighter. I can see him now in my mind's eye.'

'Who else was at the table?' Ted asked.

Paul closed his eyes.

'Joe, Nell. Jim breakfasted early and left as I came in. He had to do something to a canoe.'

'Do you know why the lighter is important?'

'Sally told me. It must have been put there deliberately—where it was found. Someone doesn't like Rowland.'

'Not necessarily,' Miss Pink said, 'they could be indifferent to him but wanting to shift attention from themselves.'

'That's a bit of an understatement, isn't it?'

'It happens more often than you think.' Ted helped himself to brandy and served Paul absently. Miss Pink smiled amiably.

'How did you get on with Bett?' she asked.

'I hated her—but I didn't kill her.'

'I know—' He glanced at her quickly. '—You were in the bar. Why did you hate her?'

'She said absolutely revolting things about Charles and me. We just happened to like going to the Schooner; sometimes we went out with Dawson fishing. She found out about it and created hell. What I found most obscene was that I got the impression she didn't really mind what Charles did or who his friends were; she was just wringing all the enjoyment out of the situation that she could. She loved scenes; she was always looking for diversions and if there weren't any, she invented them.'

'Did you stop going to the Schooner with Charles after she found out?'

'Yes, we thought we'd better for the sake of peace.'

'When did this happen?'

'About a month ago. Poor old Charles. He drinks, you know, but he *was* drinking with us, after that he started drinking on his own. It was too bad.'

He drank his brandy at a gulp and stared at the table.

'The others will be wondering where I am,' he muttered.

'The others?' Miss Pink exclaimed.

'Yes, we're all out in the hall; we couldn't stand Plas Mawr tonight.'

'Then who's on duty?'

'Sally.'

'For goodness sake! Why?'

'It should be Rowland on duty tonight—and she wanted to be doing something, I think. The kids have come along with her, and Linda's there too.'

'Perhaps it's the best thing for Sally,' she admitted after he'd gone, 'now why on earth did he tell us that rigmarole about Charles Martin?'

'To put himself in the clear; besides, how does he know that Martin hasn't talked, or that she didn't leave a diary or some other record—with details? Do you think she would blackmail them?'

'But Paul's got an alibi.' She told him what she had learned from Miss Devereux.

Ted was in a carping mood: 'He certainly couldn't have got from here to the cove on foot in half an hour, but that works only on the premise that she was killed before eleven, and for that we're depending on Hughes' story.' He was silent for a moment. 'We keep coming back to the problem of transport. Wright had none. Nell and Slade were in her van. But I wonder what Lithgow's alibi is.'

'Of course, Slade and Nell were pub-crawling. That leaves only him.'

In the few seconds that it took to pass from the dining room to the hall Miss Pink regretted the perhaps undesirable objectivity of the cosy dinner table and realised with astonishment that until this moment she hadn't really faced the fact that the killer must be a member of the small community at Plas Mawr; she had always held the hope that the possibility was nothing more than a device: a fixed point from which the investigation must make a start. Once school staff had been eliminated the net would to cast wider. Factors which pointed to a murderer in the school, motive for instance, even the theft of the lighter, these she hadn't accepted as conclusive (she realised now); she knew that acceptable explanations could be found for the most bizarre situations.

In a similar way that dreamers can span long periods in a few seconds because the brain acts like a computer and, from a memory bank of total recall, delivers an impression that is a distillation of the relevant events, so, in a few steps along a passage, five days of life and the lives of a handful of people (so far as she had knowledge of them) were processed and, as Ted held the door for her and she walked towards the small group by the fire, she felt that one of them was a murderer. She was imaginative but not fanciful. She wouldn't have said that there was a miasma of fear in the room but as a nightmare differs from a bad dream in that only the first implies panic, so she knew that the common factor between bad dreams and this moment was the sense of menace. Someone in the room was taking her measure. As she sat, and innocuous remarks were exchanged, she was aware of one emergent fact: the only person who they knew had command of transport on Saturday night and who hadn't volunteered an alibi was Lithgow—who used the Centre's Land Rover to go home.

Olwen appeared and accepted an order with the lack of expression she would use only on the most formal occasions. Miss Pink observed the others.

Lithgow and Slade looked unusually neat and conventional in shirts and ties and jackets of good Welsh tweed. Nell wore a dress in burnt orange with shoes the same colour and dark brown tights. Round her neck was a leather thong with a copper beech leaf between her breasts. She looked cool and beautiful and Miss Pink wondered how much the girl knew about Lithgow. He was saying in answer to a question from Ted that the weather forecast was poor and that tomorrow they would keep the boys low. He was referring to the expedition which would start the following morning and end at tea time on Friday. This exercise, the climax of the course, would be unaccompanied, the boys doing their own navigation but the instructors manning check points at selected sites. There were two ranges to traverse, the boys working back to the Centre from the dropping point in the north to which they'd be taken by coach.

The directors listened with only half their attention to Lithgow's account of recent modifications to the programme and from these mental sidelines they watched as a discussion developed concerning the earliest date that ice axes should be taken on the hill during these expeditions. They displayed a morbid humour as they recalled long falls down snow slopes.

Miss Pink, leaning back in her chair, wondered what they were up to. Paul looked disgruntled, Lithgow was at his most mischievous, and the other two, Nell and Slade, seemed to be abetting him. There was an atmosphere of hysteria in the group.

After letting them have their heads for a while Ted, smiling his foxy grin, said urbanely:

'We're trying to trace when Rowland lost his cigarette lighter. Can anyone help?'

The words dried up chatter and artifice like a sponge. Slade glared; Lithgow's lips thinned without smiling but his eyes danced and he didn't look at anyone in particular. Nell was suddenly grave and quiet.

'I've been thinking about it,' she said, 'of course, when a man's been a smoker since you've known him, it's difficult to remember when he started lighting his cigarettes by a different method. And where something as ordinary as smoking's concerned, it carries no impact.'

'No one else smoked,' Ted pointed out.

'Meaning he should stand out? Perhaps we got used to him, even blocked it out, which would make recall more difficult.' She smiled and shrugged, glancing at Lithgow.

'I can't remember,' he said.

Paul said defiantly: 'He had it Monday at breakfast time.'

'Did he?' Nell asked with interest. 'Well, who was with him after that?'

'I was,' Lithgow said, 'we did the canoe trip. He wouldn't have smoked in a canoe.'

'On the way to Porth Bach perhaps,' Ted said, 'in the Land Rover.'

'I don't remember.'

'I don't see how it's important,' Slade said aggressively.

'Of course it is,' Nell turned on him, speaking with the easy familiarity of one who often took him to task for being obtuse. 'The lighter was found by the passing-place. If Rowland had it Monday, either it was stolen and put there, or he went back himself.'

'How much do you know about it?' Ted asked pleasantly.

135

'Most of it,' Nell smiled. 'The kitchen staff are full of it, and we talk among ourselves. How often does a murder happen in an adventure centre? Sally's told us about the lighter and, of course, she wants us to remember seeing it after Saturday. . . . To be quite honest, we knew so much already, I mean *before* Bett disappeared,' her eyes flickered over Paul, 'that what's happened since seems almost like filling in gaps.'

'What d'you mean by that?' Paul was leaning forward, gripping the arms of his chair.

'Why, relationships. . . .' She spun the word out, staring at him. 'I meant Rowland and Bett; was there something else?'

Slade said with a surprising grin: 'He thought you meant him being pals with Charlie.'

Paul went white.

'For goodness sake!' Nell said impatiently. 'That was all Bett's doing! You *are* a fool, Joe,' she frowned at him in exasperation. 'I explained that to you at the time—'

Lithgow gave a curious snigger.

'Don't take any notice of Joe,' Nell told Paul. She looked across at the directors with the flustered air of a hen trying to collect chicks: 'Bett made a lot of trouble at the time: a whispering campaign. We didn't take any notice.'

'Did she?' Paul breathed. 'The bitch! If I'd known I'd—'

'Fortunately,' Nell went on loudly, 'the instructors stuck together; we hadn't any time for Bett and not much for Charles. You might say we ran the Centre, under Jim, and Charles just limped along behind.'

'It was an easy enough place to run,' Lithgow admitted. 'You can work up a rhythm with good staff.'

Olwen came in to tell Ted that he was wanted on the telephone.

'Do you know what's happening?' Nell asked Miss Pink.

'No, nothing more than you.'

They went on to talk about the next course in a desultory fashion. Nell was unenthusiastic; most of the students would be police cadets and these were unpopular at the Centre. 'Poor physique,' the girl explained. 'They're not hard like the boys on this course. You've got to watch police all the time on the hill; they've got no resistance. Their officers are a bad example; there were some in the Saracen's on Saturday. You saw them, Jim.' She glanced at Lithgow and he nodded. 'Why is it military personnel are so much harder than police? Is it diet?'

They started to chatter again, about food and exercise and physical types, until Miss Pink, curious to know who had telephoned Ted, took the chance to excuse herself and went upstairs. His door opened before she reached it.

'Hughes is still with them,' he said, standing aside for her to enter.

'You told them Paul remembered the lighter?'

'And gave them Sally's information about the alibi but I'm afraid they're strongly in favour of collusion. It happens, you know.'

'I do know, but not in this case, I think. And they think Paul's in collusion too?' She appropriated Ted's easy chair. 'That was a curious scene downstairs between Nell and him. Is Master Paul quite so honest as he seemed in the dining room? There could be more to it than appeared when he told it. But if there was collusion between Sally and Hughes over the lighter, it would have to include Paul.'

'And Hughes doesn't like Paul, so why should the boy lie—except for Sally's sake—'

'No,' Miss Pink said, 'I don't think anyone's lying about the lighter—oh, someone is, but not Sally or Paul.'

'Well, the police don't agree with you. There's news about Martin, however. If he isn't in the clear, he's certainly no deeper. They must have more men on the job, not counting the chaps keeping guard on the Porth Bach road. Martin's been drinking with Dawson this evening. Their conversation was quite innnocent and above-board.'

'Did Pryce have a man in the bar?'

'No, the Schooner's closed for the season. He says the room they were in was on the ground floor and there was a window open.'

'Gracious!' Miss Pink glanced at the drawn curtains.

'It's gone some way towards clearing Martin,' Ted pointed out. 'Incidentally, I told Pryce about your visit to Mrs Wolkoff and he wants to see her, too. This morning he thought she was senile; he changed his mind since he talked to headquarters about her. She was out this afternoon when he telephoned.'

'How does he account for that lighter being found at the passing-place if he thinks Hughes is lying?'

'He thinks Hughes went back to clean up, to see that he hadn't dropped anything.'

'And dropped his lighter! Pryce is mad.'

'It's only got Hughes' prints on it—apart from yours.'

'Of course, he was fiddling with it in the kitchen.'

They lapsed into a morose silence from which Miss Pink said without animation:

'About that affair of Lithgow's: it must have been Bett, not Nell, and I've been thinking about a curious remark he made to Linda when she threatened him with divorce. He said "that won't be necessary now" or something similar.'

'This was Sunday morning?'

'When she told me; he said it on Saturday night, I believe. The point is, Bett was dead when he said it but only the murderer knew that. Is that what made him say divorce wouldn't be necessary?'

'But Linda retracted the following day.'

'No, she didn't retract; she merely substituted Nell in the name part, as it were. If Lithgow killed Bett and then discovered that Linda had told me he'd been having an affair with her, he'd want to deny any association so he'd persuade Linda to change the story—or rather, the principal character.'

'Linda would guess why as soon as the body was found.'

'Isn't it a feature of sex murders that the killers are often protected by other women?'

'That's true—and a feature of this case is the wives' loyalty, with the exception of the dead one. But Lithgow a sex murderer!'

'And after all, Nell mentioned this evening that Lithgow was in the Saracen's Head on Saturday night!'

Ted pondered for a moment.

'I'd like to do some checking tomorrow,' he said, 'we'll go to the Saracen's and I'll also call on Mrs Wolkoff. She must know more than she's told you; I can't believe, from what you said, that anything could happen in that cove without her knowledge.'

'But it didn't happen there; the Jaguar is over a mile from Porth Bach—unless Bett went down to the cove to turn round after all. For Mrs Wolkoff to know anything it would have to take place near her house. The old lady couldn't be harbouring anyone I suppose: like an escaped train robber or someone waiting to get over to Ireland? I think this morning there was someone else in the cove.'

'Like the mine?' he asked.

'Imagination plays tricks,' she admitted, 'and I'm not certain about the mine, although a stone did drop in the loom and I'm pretty sure that young man was trying to distract my attention—'

'The lorries,' he interrupted, 'they've found two more.'

'At Clapham?'

'No. In Somerset, in the Mendips.'

'Caves again. Had these run off the road?'

'No, they were abandoned in a barn; they were very low on petrol.'

'It doesn't show much foresight, does it? To run out of petrol.'

'On the contrary, they'd probably served their purpose.'

'There's still one missing.'

'I expect it's waiting to be found. Like to take a bet on its whereabouts?'

'No. It could be anywhere in limestone country. South Wales perhaps.'

Chapter Twelve

MISS PINK WAS wrong. At eight o'clock the following morning the radio announcer said that the fourth lorry had been found in a wood near Clapham. It was a minor news item and probably only included because now all the vehicles had been recovered. So that was that, she thought, wondered briefly where the drivers were, and then applied herself to the business of the day: breakfast first, then the renewed search for information, starting with Lithgow's alibi.

The Saracen's Head was in Bontddu, about fifteen miles north of Bethel and approached by a tortuous route which contoured below the satellite hills of Yr Aran. The road was narrow and, once the coastal plain was left behind, ran through huge gorges where occasional rock faces impended above them heralded by notices warning motorists to beware of falling stones.

The gorges were wooded with old gnarled oaks and fine conifers, the latter giving an alpine atmosphere to the country, enhanced by a brawling torrent in the bottom which was noted for its salmon. The road followed the river and progress was slow. Short of using a helicopter there was no way of travelling fast between the coast and the Saracen's Head.

At ten o'clock in the off-season the hotel was a bright and cheerless place, whitewashed, with imitation leaded windows and frosted nasturtiums wilting in the flower beds. The manager was French, or rather he spoke with a French accent and sported a Van Dyke beard; he disowned all knowledge of the public bar but the questioners were bland and difficult to dismiss. In the end he capitulated and gave them the address of the barman whom, he added as a parting shot, they would find in bed.

The river flowed through the town and its banks were bordered by a miscellany of houses. There were one or two large Victorian edifices, built of stone and slate with hideous facings of yellow brick, and charming lawned gardens sloping to the river; and there were terraces of holiday cottages with pastel paint and picture windows among which the occasional indigenous house showed up like a rotting stump in a set of gleaming dentures.

They knocked at a peeling door several times before it was opened by a pale fat man with a red beard and dissipated eyes. He had a bad cold and, as the manager had foretold, had plainly just got out of his bed. They apologised for disturbing him and asked if he could spare them a moment.

He led the way along a narrow passage that was further encumbered by a sideboard and a bicycle and appeared to be paved with broken quarry tiles and plastic toys. There was a strong smell of Friar's Balsam.

In a back room with no picture window and the river glimpsed through old iron bedsteads which formed the garden fence, where all the chairs were covered by unidentified and rather smelly clothing and there was no place to sit, their host, who turned out to be a Londoner married to a Welsh woman, thought about the previous Saturday evening. They described Lithgow and Nell but it wasn't until they said that Slade looked like a boxer that the barman's face showed interest and he waved a dirty hand at Miss Pink:

'Yers, I know *'im,* seen 'im thump a chap once, cor'—there was three on 'em. No one come up for more of the same. Bin in the Commandos, I think. Slade, you say 'is name was? Got a plain looking bird with nice legs. *They* was in Sat'day and, yers, you're right, they was with this other chap, now I come to think: Scotch, wi' queer eyes, works at the same place. They was in late Sat'day, near closing time.'

'Ten-thirty?'

He shot them a suspicious glance. It occurred to Miss Pink that he thought they were trying to trap him into admitting he sold drinks outside permitted hours.

'They was in about ten-thirty,' he said sullenly.

He could tell them nothing else. It was a Saturday night and the busiest hour of the week. Although the hotels were nearly empty in November, the area still attracted a large number of climbers and walkers who would camp, or sleep in huts and fill the bars in the evening. He couldn't remember when they came in, how long they were there, nor if they came separately. All he could say was that he'd seen them, around ten-thirty.

A pound note changed hands.

'Waste of money,' Ted commented when they were back in the car.

'Not at all,' she retorted, 'he didn't see Lithgow before ten-thirty. If that is the earliest *anyone* saw him, where was he before that? He could have killed Bett after Hughes left the Jaguar and, if he knew in advance that Nell and Slade would be in Bontddu, he had ample time to drive here before ten-thirty and establish an alibi.'

'But he hasn't established one. As you say, he had ample time. In any case—establishing an alibi: that sounds premeditated. I've got the feeling this murder wasn't.'

'I agree. But if not premeditated, what on earth would Lithgow be doing on the cliffs on a wet Saturday evening? Dropping some equipment to do with the canoe expeditions, or picking it up? Mrs Wolkoff would know, I'll be bound.'

As they returned to the coast she took a 2½-inch map out of her pocket and studied it. There was a path which left the main road about three quarters of a mile inland from Porth Bach and ran across the fields to the cove. They decided to approach Mrs Wolkoff's cottage by this route.

They left the car in a lay-by and discovered the start of the track marked by an old stone stile with dressed rock for steps and a large slate placed as an additional obstruction to sheep at the top. The field wall was massive with a bank of earth on top, very similar to the walls of Land's End, except that the rock wasn't granite.

The presence of the stile put paid to any theory that Porth

Bach was accessible to vehicles other than by the road along the top of the cliffs.

The way led across bleak and treeless fields, mostly pasture, but occasionally a few Friesian cows were feeding on kale behind an electric fence. Farm buildings showed up distinctly in the soft light although there was no sun, and white-washed structures were dazzling. The track ran below walls for the most part, skirting farmsteads with curious names: Rififi and Corn and Nant y Pig; and here and there a green swelling was identified on the map as a burial chamber or ancient fort.

The sea showed ahead and below and the path dipped. Trees appeared: hawthorns, then sycamores and oaks. Under the trees the path was muddy and they saw with interest what they had noticed at the stiles: that many walkers, at least, many people with cleated boots, had passed this way and recently.

'The local field club's had an outing,' Ted said, 'and destroyed all the evidence.'

'You think that's what it is?'

'I know; they were out on Sunday. I saw it in the local paper. But they went east from the cove, as the canoes did on Monday, so they couldn't have seen the Jaguar.'

Occasionally they came on telephone poles bearing the line to the cove. They found the cottage quite suddenly because in the depths of the wooded ravine they had little idea how close they were to the shore. No smoke rose from the chimney.

'She's out again,' Miss Pink said morosely. Then they saw the bag.

It was a plastic carrier, blue and white, from the Co-op. It was hanging from an ornamental knob in the middle of the front door. They looked inside. There were two letters and a typewritten note to the postman telling him that the writer would be away for a week or so and to leave the mail in the bag. The addresses on the letters were typed. One had a Plymouth postmark and the other came from Cardiff.

'Very careless, to advertise her absence like this,' Miss Pink muttered, 'I didn't think she was a careless woman.'

She stepped aside and peered through the living room window. What she could see of the interior appeared no different from what she had seen yesterday. The room on the other side of the double-fronted house would be the parlour. Apart from the fact that it had a tiny genteel grate instead of a range, there was little difference between this and the living room. There was a table and a sideboard facing the window with a huge looking glass from which their faces peered back at them owlishly, and every flat surface was covered by the ubiquitous files and books and newspapers.

They stepped back and looked at the upstairs windows. These were tightly closed but the curtains were drawn back. Miss Pink led the way round the side of the house to the back door which, as they'd expected, was locked or bolted. There was a window which showed them a poky little kitchen and another, very cobwebbed on the inside, that was just too high to look through.

There was a chopping-block by the backdoor, a saw-horse and an orange-crate. While she steadied the crate, Ted tried to see through the window.

'It's too dirty to see anything,' he grumbled, rubbing a hand over the panes, 'I suppose this is salt on the glass—hello!' There was a click. He stepped down as if he'd been bitten.

'What did you do?'

'I don't think it's fastened properly.'

'Isn't it?' Her eyes gleamed. 'You hold the crate.'

She climbed up and pushed the window. It gave, then sagged towards her slightly as she removed her hand. It was an old window, hinged at the side, and partially secured by a rusting arm with holes in it. She knew, because she had a similar window in her own house, that the catch was broken.

She sent Ted to find a tool and after a while he returned with a broken hack-saw blade. She inserted it skilfully, eased the arm off its peg and the window gaped wide.

'Should one of us watch for the police?' she asked.

'We might as well both go in; I know you won't stay outside, and I'm your accomplice if you do the entering, so let's go.'

They lugged the saw-horse to the window and with some

difficulty, because the opening was small, they climbed inside to find themselves in a dark narrow place hung with decrepit mackintoshes, and with old tins of paint, polish, cleaning fluid, on a makeshift shelf. They moved hesitantly towards the living quarters. At the opposite end of the cupboard-like space a door gave access to the kitchen. This appeared unremarkable with a Calor-gas stove and cylinder, cupboards and shelves, a small table covered with American cloth and a sink with a metal draining board. There were no dirty dishes. The sink tidy had been emptied and rinsed clean.

Another door led out of the kitchen and into the living room. She glanced round, trying to see if anything had been changed, re-arranged. She thought not. Even the ashes in the fireplace looked the same. She couldn't speak for all the contents of the table but a *Daily Telegraph* colour supplement which had been lying behind the typewriter was in the same position.

Like the other rooms, the parlour was no more unusual than it appeared from outside.

The stairs went up from the front door. They mounted slowly but firmly, Miss Pink first. She felt cold and sick.

They looked into both bedrooms, at first flinching in anticipation, then boldly. The bedsteads were both of brass and the beds were made up neatly, with candlewick quilts. Each room had chairs, a wardrobe, and a chest of drawers. One room was obviously Mrs Wolkoff's. On the bedside table were a Bible and a book called *The Health Seeker*, a powerful torch and the telephone.

In a corner of the ceiling was a trap-door. Ted stood on a chair and lifted the trap. A shower of dust and rubble enveloped them. Miss Pink handed him the torch and he inspected the loft, then he lowered the trap and descended. 'Nothing,' he said.

'It's a good thing that what you thought hasn't happened,' he remarked when they were downstairs again, 'we've left fingerprints everywhere.'

'Why should you speculate on what I was thinking? We can alibi each other,' she said absently, walking into the kitchen. 'No fridge,' she went on, opening cupboards, 'shelves for groceries, bread bin—no bread, biscuit tins for butter and fats, more biscuit tins—empty, but cake crumbs here; cheese dish, empty. She cleared up carefully so that nothing would go bad while she was away. Was she a vegetarian? No. Bovril here, and a tin of sausages. Now where did she keep bacon and meat?'

She stood back and looked at the cooker, stepped forward, tried the screw on top of the cylinder. 'Very prudent woman: remembered to turn off the gas.' She opened the oven door. 'What's this?'

'What's that?' Ted asked from the living room.

She didn't answer. He came to the doorway as she was turning from the open oven with a roasting tin in her hands. Something was in the tin wrapped in foil.

She unwrapped the foil to expose half a leg of lamb, raw.

They had hoped to find the police above Puffin Cove but the place was deserted and there was nothing to show of the crime except the marks in the turf made by the Jaguar.

'You'd think he'd leave someone on guard,' Ted said testily, 'not that anyone's likely to come here in winter.'

'There was a patrol car at the junction yesterday.'

'That explains it. They'll be short-handed with the explosives bother and a car at the road-end is as much as they can manage. I feel we should let Pryce know about that meat as soon as we can,' he urged as his companion showed unexpected interest in the clumps of gorse beside the road.

'You go on to the patrol car,' she told him, 'I'll follow. I've thought of something.'

When he'd left she spent some time walking among the bushes and moving slowly up and down the tarmac near where the lighter had been found. Then she strolled back to the lip of the main cove and sat on a boulder, staring down at Porth Bach. At last she nodded to herself and got up and walked along the cliff road to the Schooner, so engrossed that she didn't notice there was no police car at the junction.

Dawson of the Schooner was a surprising little man who

resembled the post-war "spiv". He was dark and dapper in flannels, blazer and silk cravat and he wore a toothbrush moustache. He looked as if he had got stuck in a style that was a quarter of a century out of date. He was anxious to please and talked breathlessly in accents that reminded Miss Pink of a politician who had been taking elocution lessons.

Ted had come to the hotel to make his call and Dawson had lent him an old van so that he could go to meet the police. Superintendent Pryce wanted to see him. Miss Pink's expression betrayed her for he admitted that he couldn't help overhearing the conversation since the telephone was in his sitting room. As he talked he ushered her into a pleasant bar with prints of sailing ships on the walls and in one corner a splendid gaudy figurehead. He switched on an electric heater. Through a wide window there was a glorious view of the bay.

She drank sherry while her host prattled on about the murder and she admired the sweep of cliffs from the headland on which the hotel was built to its opposite point beyond which lay the estuary. The voice penetrated her consciousness:

'—would never do a thing like that, never!'

'What?' She turned. 'I'm so sorry, your view takes one's breath away; you were saying?'

'Mrs Wolkoff would never go away and leave a joint in the oven. She had independent means but with inflation—you know how it is for people with fixed incomes: she had to be very careful. A joint would be a luxury to her, a special treat. She'd never buy lamb just before she was going away and then forget it!'

'That's what I thought,' she said, 'and I'm sure the police will take the same view. It's occurred to me that you're in a similar position to Mrs Wolkoff. No, no—' he had shot her an alarmed look, '—I don't mean you're about to disappear at any moment but that you're in a situation geographically which commands the whole of the bay. Haven't you seen anything—curious, recently?'

'No,' he confessed with regret, 'I don't use this room in winter you see, except at Christmas when friends come in for drinks.

147

My bedroom faces the same way but, of course, the curtains are drawn at night. My kitchen and sitting room face inland and towards the west respectively.'

'Disappointing. Seeing that the hotel is so obvious from Porth Bach, I'd anticipated you would have the area under surveillance.' She smiled to take any sting out of the words.

The smile had its effect. Dawson was concerned that she should think him not conversant with the local traffic.

'Of course, I know what goes on there from Mrs Wolkoff, also from my own observations when I'm out fishing, but I'm talking generally, and there's never been anything *sinister*, you know?'

'What goes on there?' she asked casually.

'Well now, where does one start?' He came from behind the bar carrying his glass and the bottle of Tio Pepe. He took a chair and they sat companionably staring out at the calm expanse of sea and the reddish cliffs. 'The three cottages other than Mrs Wolkoff's are owned, first, by a surgeon from London called Silkin; they only let to friends. Theirs is the long cottage below Mrs Wolkoff. Then comes Miss Lupin's place. She's not young but she's very attractive, if you like that sort of thing, and beautifully made up. Most inappropriate for this part of the world. There's a rumour that the cottage was a gift. She doesn't come often but lets it—to anybody. Then there's—'

'Stop there,' Miss Pink said, 'what do you mean by "anybody"?'

'Well, I'm not a snob but Miss Lupin's friends seem to be show business people and although *they're* all right, they have hangers-on who—' he shrugged appealingly: 'well, they're not quite out of the top drawer.'

'Are you implying that sometimes the show business overlaps the criminal element?'

'Oh no!' He was horrified. 'I'd never allow criminals at the Schooner. If I knew, of course.'

'That's the rub, isn't it? Tell me about the fourth cottage.'

'That's the one nearest the jetty. It's owned by a couple called Adams: retired hoteliers who have gone to the Algarve for a year or so to see how they like it. That's let on a long lease to a chap called Davigdor who's interested in underwater archaeology. He's done some good work in the Mediterranean with Roman wrecks, I believe.'

'Are there wrecks here?'

'Ha! Reg Davigdor keeps very quiet about that, but there's a lot of exploring going on in the bay. There's a club from Anglesey is often here. We're quite crowded at times. Reg always contacts me when he's coming down so that I know they're about when I go to lift my lobster pots. I knew a chap who got caught up with a motor boat on the Riviera and had three thousand stitches. He was lucky to be alive. I wouldn't like to do that to a skin diver.'

'They operate from Porth Bach?'

'Yes, all of them. Davigdor's people and the club. It's the only access to the sea there is in the bay, except mine but that's private. Of course, anyone can approach by water. One of Reg's friends has a converted torpedo boat and he comes up occasionally.'

'What were you doing on Saturday night?'

'I had a small party which included Llewelyn, the police surgeon, and another friend of mine who's in command of a Royal Navy boat at Holyhead. And their wives. Then there was Miss Devereux who, of course, was concerned with your meal during the early part of the evening, so we dined late, about nine. For some hours before that I was dodging about between the kitchen and this room.'

'What I really meant was did you observe anything odd towards Porth Bach, but I must say, it's pleasant to find someone with such an impeccable alibi.'

'Why, don't the—'

A bell rang in the bar.

'Now who can that be?' her host asked and excused himself, leaving her to contemplate the unexpected relationship between him and Miss Devereux. She assumed that the mutual interest must be food.

He came back with Ted who had returned the van. He had

been followed to the hotel by the detectives and now he offered Miss Pink a lift.

'We're going to the cove,' he told her between the front door and the police car.

Pryce greeted her solemnly but said nothing at first about their illegal entry into the cottage. He didn't appear convinced that the joint had any sinister significance. He took the view that the old lady was as mad as a hatter, led a queer life and mixed with queer people and it was quite likely that if she'd received a telephone call and had to leave suddenly, or if someone had come to collect her in a car, that she might clear away the obvious scraps of food and forget the joint which was hidden from sight.

She noted with interest that the old lady's political activities were known to the police and she pointed out that if someone had come to pick her up in a car it would have been seen by the uniformed police at the junction.

'Not necessarily,' Pryce said, 'she could have walked up the ravine to the main road. These anarchists hop around like fleas and they get no better as they get older, if anything they become more unpredictable. She'll be in Aberystwyth or Cardiff now at some rally or just possibly looking after a sick friend, and what she'll say when she gets back and finds her house has been entered is nobody's business.'

'I doubt if she'll know,' Miss Pink said and stopped, surprised at her own assumption that after all, Mrs Wolkoff would come back. Out here in the sparkling air the joint seemed pathetic rather than sinister: Mrs Wolkoff's lost treat.

'. . . she may be mad,' Pryce was saying, 'but these old girls who live alone know if a mouse gets in, let alone people breaking and entering.'

Miss Pink thought how right he was and she didn't even trouble to point out that Mrs Wolkoff wasn't an anarchist. When they arrived at the cove she didn't walk up the ravine with them but stayed at the turning-circle looking at the ground. Ted glanced at her then followed the police.

Originally the circle would have been a clear space of bedrock and thin soil but someone, probably the local property owners, had put down several loads of shingle. Under pressure this had formed a hard surface but where pockets of soil had been deep the stones had worked down so that now they were covered by a skin of mud. There were imprints of tyres and cleated boots.

She walked down to the jetty and looked at the varnished dinghy which lay, bottom up, well above high water mark, secured to a ring bolt by a painter of nylon rope. She knelt down and tilted the boat slightly so that she could peer underneath. As she had expected, there was nothing except the shingle: no oars and no rowlocks.

She stood and stared at the Adams' cottage. The shutters were of steel and they were closed from the inside. The house possessed no outbuildings but there was a septic tank between it and the shore. She walked round it and saw pipes coming from what must be the bathroom. It was a good cottage: solid, four-square and, so far as vandals were concerned, it appeared impregnable.

She started up the ravine and on the way observed the properties belonging to the elegant Miss Lupin and the Silkins. She noted that Miss Lupin's place also had steel shutters but that its roof needed attention. On its seaward side was a walled paddock with a tumbledown barn that would once have sheltered a cow or a pony. She got into the paddock by means of a gap in the wall and entered the barn. A slit-shaped aperture in one wall commanded the jetty, the turning-circle and the Adams' cottage. Rubble and broken slates covered the floor and showed no footprints.

The Silkins' cottage stood on the other side of the stream. A lot of money had been spent on it and it was a delightful place but there was nothing remarkable about it in the present context. Like the other empty places, it had steel shutters.

The light was fading but she could just make out the police behind Mrs Wolkoff's cottage. Watched by Ted from a distance they were scuffing among the dead leaves at the edge of the wood.

'What do they think?' she asked.

'They've been inside—the same way,' he smiled. 'But they found no signs of foul play any more than we did. There hasn't been a struggle, there's no blood, everything's as neat and proper as you'd expect it to be—except for the joint.'

'And the note to the postman advertising the fact that the house was empty?'

'She couldn't have been normal to live here all on her own,' he said as if that explained everything. 'I forgot to tell you: they've let Hughes go.'

'They had to,' she said simply.

'Why?'

'Whatever was done here, he was in custody at the time.'

'So you're back to that. You won't accept it that she just forgot the joint and her absence has an innocent explanation?'

'No, none of it's in character.' She looked down the ravine. 'Steel shutters against vandals, and a valuable dinghy left out unprotected—nothing makes sense. But it's shaping: forming a very nebulous pattern. What appears to be revealing itself is fantastic and I'm quite aware that much of it is due to imagination, although what's that except being able to put yourself in the place of other people?'

'Which people?'

'I've been thinking of Bett, and Mrs Wolkoff.'

'Did you get anywhere?'

'Oh, some considerable distance, but I want to get things straight before I tell Pryce—or even you. What has he been doing this morning?'

'I met him at Plas Mawr but by the time he arrived all the instructors were out on the hill. I guess he'd wanted to have a go at Lithgow.'

'Why isn't he interested in the cliffs any longer?'

'I think he's finished down here, but there's a shortage of manpower too. Dawson said the police car was at the junction this morning but it left before we arrived. There's a flap over security at the mine and I think that in the circumstances the murder's taken second place.'

152

On the way back from the coast Pryce said they would do nothing about the old lady for the time being; they couldn't, he said petulantly, on the strength of half a leg of lamb. Miss Pink didn't seem concerned; she continued to look out of the window at the line of mountains. Once she remarked that the cloud was dropping. She frowned as she said this and Ted assumed that she was thinking about the boys on the tops.

Chapter Thirteen

I T W A S A bright, brassy dawn and at eight o'clock the weather forecast was bad. None of the instructors heard it; four of them were checking the boys out of the camp sites where they'd spent the night, and Nell Harvey was eating a hurried breakfast at Plas Mawr. The high-level route had been chosen after all and she was to man the first check point: the summit of Moel Eilio which was just under three thousand feet at the end of a long ridge running north-west from Yr Aran.

At eight o'clock Miss Pink was also eating a solitary breakfast. By eight-thirty she was in her car and heading for the Schooner. She was in climbing clothes and beside her was a small rucksack which contained the usual items of mountaineering equipment: elastoplast, maps, a torch, spare sweaters and two packed lunches.

There was no sun; the too-bright dawn had given way to a milky cloud cover which, over the hills, held strange, unshadowed depths. The tops were clear and hard like cardboard. Occasionally a snowflake landed on the windscreen and melted immediately.

Dawson was evidently an early riser. He was dressed and shaved when he came to the front door but he was astonished to see his visitor. Miss Pink wasted no time on preliminaries.

'There's a rowing boat on the shore at Porth Bach in good condition,' she said, 'a varnished boat. Do you know it?'

'That belongs to the Adams. The oars are kept in the cottage.'

'The boat has been used recently. The weed marking the last high tide has been disturbed and there are other marks in the sandy patches. Someone has raked them over to try to conceal the groove the boat made.'

'Davidgor wasn't down last weekend so far as I know,' he said slowly, watching her. 'He didn't phone me anyway and I'd have noticed them if they'd been out on Sunday.'

'I don't think those marks were there on Tuesday morning,' she said. Then: 'Are there any caves in the bay?'

'I'll show you.' He led the way to the room which looked towards the east and crossed to the window. 'There are no caves as such east of Porth Bach,' he told her, 'depressions, but not true caves. What are you looking for?'

'A cave which has some portion above high water mark, and one that is accessible only by boat—although a dry cave is a remote possibility.'

'How big a boat?'

'The torpedo boat belonging to Davigdor's friend?'

'Oh no! Definitely not. You're no sailor, Miss Pink.'

'Elimination,' she explained. 'A cave then that is accessible to an inflatable boat or dinghy.'

'In good conditions you could go anywhere along the foot of the cliffs in boats like that. What are you thinking of? Smuggling?'

'I'm not sure; I shall know more by this evening but—caves?'

'Ah yes. There are two. One is Ogof Ddu: you can't actually see it because it faces away from us. It's between Porth Bach and Puffin Cove, just east of Puffin.' He pointed. 'Then, in Puffin itself, on the easterly side, is Ogof Lladron; that's also hidden from us by a sloping buttress: the light is picking out the crest of it now. It has a pinkish tinge.'

'I see. Lladron means "thieves".'

'Does it? It sounds as if it had a history then, but I don't know the story. What kind of smuggling do you think? Spirits, or something nasty, like drugs?'

She looked at him thoughtfully.

'Drugs take up such a small space,' she murmured, 'on the other hand accessibility could be more important than space. Where is your launch?'

'Down below. I've got a mooring that's sheltered from everything but an easterly gale. If that's forecast I take her over to

155

Porth Bach and use a mooring of Silkin's. I'll have to watch the wind today.'

'I'd like to go and look at these two caves. Would it be convenient for us to go today, as soon as possible?'

He was delighted. He had been meaning to lift his lobster pots but they could wait till the afternoon. He hurried away and returned very quickly in stained flannels and a seaman's jersey. He carried a heavy torch and a pair of rowlocks.

The anchorage was a gouge in the eastern side of the headland. It wasn't a cove for there was no beach; at high tide the sea would wash the foot of the cliffs which were about two hundred feet high. Access was immediately below the hotel where there was a kind of twisting rake with steps cut in the rock and an iron handrail: a sensational way, but safe.

On the opposite side of the anchorage there was a magnificent syncline with long, diagonal strata sloping down to a shelf on the water-line. It was about two hours after high tide and huge platforms were exposed at the foot of the cliffs. These were on different levels and covered with a thin veneer of what looked like black slime.

The rock below the hotel was less firm than that on the syncline. On the staircase itself all the loose stuff had been cleared away but on either side there were tottering flakes and pinnacles and, in one place, a large detached block stood poised on the outside of the steps.

'Don't touch that,' Dawson warned, 'it's balanced on nothing.' At the foot of the staircase a small fibre-glass dinghy lay high and dry, but still carefully secured, on one of the upper shelves. She helped him manoeuvre it into the sea and was surprised at its lightness. This was essential, he told her, because usually he handled it alone and at this state of the tide it had to be lowered the last few feet down a sloping gully by a system of ropes and pulleys.

The rock staircase continued with a few steps in the outer edge of the seaward shelf, and while she held the painter Dawson went back to a cleft in the cliff and withdrew a pair of oars.

They rowed out to the launch and secured the dinghy at the

stern. Dawson's lobster boat was a half-decked craft with a capacious well for the pots. While he concerned himself with the engine Miss Pink had a chance to look at the weather.

On a clear day Yr Aran and the rest of the range would be visible across the bay but now all the mountains were obscured by an opaque and pearly film. The air was sticky and still.

By the time they were under way and heading towards Porth Bach the Merioneth coast was concealed behind the same kind of murk that hid the mountains. But the sea remained calm and Dawson reckoned that they would have a good two or three hours clear before they might have to look for shelter. Since they couldn't be more than two miles from Porth Bach and its good anchorage at any time there was no cause for alarm.

As they neared Puffin Cove Miss Pink studied the scene with interest. Since it was some hours short of low water there was no sign of the Jaguar but they could see a fresh scar on the top of the cliff where the car had touched before it bounded clear.

In the cove itself one saw that at high tide the cliffs would drop straight into the sea but now there were massive boulders at their foot for the rock was soft and unstable and these would be eroded blocks that had fallen from above.

There were few birds about: no gulls, but occasional fulmars glided past, looking for food with soft black eyes like gentle cats. There was something uncanny about this silent flight and the absence of calls, and Miss Pink found herself wishing for the raucous gulls.

There were no other birds except for the odd shag drying its wings on a rock.

The launch chugged gently under the cliffs, the first snow drifted to the deck and she had a sudden reversion of feeling. She looked at those terrible rounded boulders, thought of bruised shins and sprained ankles, of her arthritis—and she wondered why she was there.

Dawson anchored off Ogof Ddu and she regarded the cave with distaste. Then from her rucksack she produced her head-light which she fastened over her balaclava. The flex was clipped to the back of the headland and then ran down her back to the battery in her anorak pocket. Her arms and hands were thus free. Dawson, who was wearing a short oilskin which he'd brought up from the cabin, put his torch in the pouch.

They rowed ashore—if the boulders could be termed shore. It was the worst terrain that Miss Pink had ever come across. The rocks were too close for them to make a way between, and so slimy that to get on top and jump from one to the next would have been to invite a broken leg in a matter of seconds. They progressed by clambering over, and round and through the gaps, to be further frustrated by the fact that they could find no purchase for their hands. They said nothing, but slipped and grasped and fumbled, taking about ten minutes to cover a few yards, then the walls of the chasm were above them and surprisingly, for she hadn't looked ahead, the boulders ended in a sloping shingle beach.

They scrunched up the wet stones into gloom that was loud with the drip of water. The cave wasn't very deep and the daylight penetrated almost to the back of it except for shadows in the roof. The two torch beams lit these corners powerfully but it was quite obvious, if not to Dawson, then to Miss Pink who knew something of the nature of rock, that there was no formation beyond the reach of their lights that could conceal anything larger than a matchbox. What they were looking for had to be considerably bigger than that, otherwise why choose a cave? There must be thousands of inaccessible hiding places on the face of the cliffs which would hold a small object.

'How are drugs kept dry?' Dawson asked curiously as they made their way back to the dinghy, but Miss Pink, feeling ineffectual, and bruised and battered into the bargain, for once affected not to hear.

Ogof Lladron was on the other side of the buttress that formed the eastern headland of Puffin Cove. Probably the two caves were part of the same fault. The cove was sandy at the back and would have made a good landing place but for its total inaccessibility from the land. She saw that there were several lines up the cliff that might tempt a good rock climber but the rock was loose and, in any event, such routes provided no access in the normal sense of the term.

The floor of the cave was submerged and since there were no ledges along the walls, entrance could be effected only by boat.

Dawson turned round in the mouth and rowed forward so that now they could both see where they were going.

Water slapped eerily in the depths and, as in Ogof Ddu, the gloom was punctuated by the sound of drips.

'Does it dry out at low tide?' Miss Pink asked.

'I don't know if it does at the back. The entrance is always covered. I've never been in here before. It isn't my kind of place at all.'

The torch beams probed the darkness, Miss Pink obtaining extra power by shining Dawson's along the beam of her own.

'There's what looks like a ledge high up,' she said, but he had seen it at the same time.

'That will be where the shag nest,' he told her, 'they're always flying in here in the season.'

The back if the cave ended abruptly in a wet, concave wall that gleamed in the light, and the roof ran down to meet it so that the end of the cavern would be completely filled at high tides. The only ledge was the one that they'd seen; on the other side the wall curved smoothly into the water without a break.

Dawson turned the dinghy and started back towards the entrance. Miss Pink studied the rock below the ledge.

'There!' she said suddenly, 'if you can get the boat close to the rock, there's a line of holds leading up to the ledge.'

'*You* can't go up that!' he protested, 'it's sheer!'

'It's nothing of the sort—and it's only a matter of twenty feet or so. You must move the boat away once I've stepped on the rock because if I do come off I prefer to fall in the water rather than on something hard.'

'You'll catch pneumonia!'

'Nonsense. It's an easy climb and if I fall in you can row me back to the launch and I'll change into that spare clothing you've got in the cabin.'

He pulled close to the rock and, reaching over the side, found a barnacled pocket by which he could hold them in. The rock was plentifully supplied with these pockets and her only difficulty was the high step out of the rocking boat but she was, despite her age, a powerful woman and, using her arms and shoulders, she pulled herself on to the rock and the boat bobbed up behind her like a cork. She directed her beam up the line of holds.

'That's fine,' she said, 'now you pull back a few feet out of the way, and don't worry if I come off: I'm a good swimmer.'

He watched in amazement as she climbed what was indeed vertical rock, but without the advantage of a climber's experience he had no idea of the security provided by large holds and he found it quite unaccountable that a woman who must be twenty years his senior could accomplish something that he knew would have been beyond him.

Miss Pink didn't make the mistake of trying to stand when she reached the ledge, but looked up first. She was sensible; a secondary roof impended about three feet above her head and exploration could be furthered only by what in climbing parlance is termed a stomach traverse. There was a strong smell of fish-eating birds.

She directed her torch to the left, towards the back of the cave, but there the ledge ran out after only a few yards. To the right there appeared to be a break where the wall jutted forward to block the passage but she thought that the ledge was considerably longer than the few yards that were visible and that it must continue beyond the projection. From below Dawson confirmed this.

The traverse to the corner was easy. The ledge was about three feet wide and, apart from the shallow depressions which had been utilised by the nesting birds, level. She reached the corner and further easy progress was barred but, reaching up to the roof, she found a fine horizontal crack where roof and wall met and, leaning out on this, she could see footholds under the ledge which would enable her to work round the obstruction. The water looked much more than twenty feet below.

Rock climbing, particularly in gloom and unfamiliar surroundings, needs all one's concentration even when the crux has been passed, because that is when the climber, relaxing, is most vulnerable and likely to fall. But she had been trained in a hard school and didn't relax until she was safe on the continuation of the ledge again, squinting along it to the entrance and the sea. So, with her attention focused towards the daylight, she almost missed the dark niche which was a kind of reverse of the projecting corner. She noticed it because it was a black space on the fringe of the torchlight: space where there should be rock wall. She turned her head so that the beam shone into the shallow cavity.

The rock walls gleamed and the floor was matt, not white with bird droppings because these were covered by the matt substance: clothing, but it wasn't clothing only, it was Mrs Wolkoff.

Perhaps they were in the cave for an hour and a half but it seemed like another day when they emerged and rowed towards the launch. The sea was still fairly quiet which was just as well for the snow was falling thickly and with anything more than the thin breeze which was now blowing they would have had a blizzard.

Aboard the launch, Dawson headed straight for the hotel but once they came out from the shelter of the cliffs his preoccupation with Mrs Wolkoff's death was superseded by concern about the weather.

'Wind's backed,' he announced, 'I'll drop you at the anchorage and you go up and phone Pryce. Then will you come and pick me up at Porth Bach? I'll take the launch there for tonight.'

She agreed and he handed her the key of the Schooner's front door.

'I don't like the idea of your going back to Porth Bach in this,' she said, wiping her spectacles.

'I'm as safe on the sea as on dry land,' he responded, and then asked the question which so far he had hesitated to ask: 'Who did it?'

She hesitated too, not from fear of slander but because of the incontestable right of a man who has not yet been proved guilty. But the unique circumstances: the tiny boat on the grey water, the strange, shifting world of the snowstorm like the inside of a paperweight, the body behind them in the dripping cave, these made her reveal the conclusions she'd reached.

'Mrs Wolkoff was killed because she knew something about Bett Martin's death,' she told him, 'and the only person who hasn't an alibi for the time *she* was killed is Lithgow.'

He didn't seem surprised and she reflected that, since Martin was his friend, he must have speculated on the identity of Bett's murderer.

'Why?' he asked. 'Drugs? It must have been, because it's got to be something very valuable to be worth two murders.'

'Oh yes, he had a very strong motive; you may depend on that. He has it still.'

Dawson glanced back towards Porth Bach, frowning. 'I wonder—is there any tie-up between Lithgow and Davigdor?'

'Why do you ask?'

'I don't know anything about Lithgow, except that the Centre's down here a lot, but I've always felt that there was something not quite right about Porth Bach. The people, I mean. Davigdor and his pals were always very well-behaved when they came to the Schooner but they didn't tell you anything about themselves. You didn't notice it at the time because they talked continuously: only about diving though. . . . I know what it was. They never got drunk!'

Their eyes met and she nodded. 'Young men?'

'Young twenties—except for Davigdor and his friend off the torpedo boat. They were older. But they were all—sort of—well-drilled.'

Miss Pink started.

'What was Davigdor like?'

'Ordinary. Quite good-looking, rather attractive in fact, but cool. Nothing really to *distinguish* him, except he'd lost a finger.'

'Which one?'

'The little finger. Let me think now.' He closed his eyes and splayed each hand in turn. 'The right—yes, the right hand.'

She saw the young Army officer sketching a salute on Sunday morning, with his right hand and the stub of a little finger.

'Be careful.' She stepped across to the weedy stairs and grasped the handrail. He nodded and pulled away into invisibility and she realised that, in addition to everything else, now they had fog to contend with, and wondered again if he would be all right. But he'd insisted that he knew what he was doing and she could only assume that her trepidation arose from her ignorance of boats. Crossing to Porth Bach must be as simple for him as the climb to the ledge had been for her.

She went up the rock staircase slowly, finding her land legs. She felt extremely tired and wondered if Pryce would want to go out to the cave tonight. At least, she thought grimly, the discovery of Mrs Wolkoff's body would focus his attention on the cove where it was needed, and quickly. She had searched the nesting ledge for the whole of its length but there was nothing else in Ogof Lladron. The dinghy had been used only to transport the body, and something else was hidden at Porth Bach which could be discovered only with a search warrant.

She was nearly at the top of the cliff when, through the sound of the sea, she heard a splatting crack on the rock behind her. There had been something else—a thud? She spun round, facing out, and slipped on the melting snow. She slithered down a few steps but even before she'd regained control she knew what had happened. She shouted: 'Look out, Dawson!' gave a loud, choked scream, not wholly simulated and, clutching the handrail, started to run silently down the staircase.

At the poised block she stopped, put her solid back against the wall and pushed hard with her feet. The block heeled over and went crashing down the cliff. It made too much noise—but perhaps it would be thought that her falling body had started a stonefall.

She continued to the sloping platform and then went left,

working round the back of the anchorage. At first her only thought was to get away from the person who had shot at her but when she stopped and listened and heard no one behind, she went more slowly and where she had acted instinctively, now her reason re-asserted itself.

Seaward, she could hear the sound of a receding engine so Dawson couldn't have heard her cries nor the crash of the falling rock, but how would the person on top interpret her shout and the sound of that engine? She had intended him to think that even if she were dead, there was someone else on the staircase. Would he assume, as she hoped, that there had been a third person in the party who was now in the launch?

If he did think there was a second person on the cliff he wouldn't expect that man to come up to the top to be shot so he would come down eventually and search the platforms. She had a few minutes' grace at most; and whatever the length of time, it wouldn't be enough if the fog cleared. She must find another way to the top and, because she was headed in that direction, at this point she remembered the syncline and its sloping strata.

It was difficult to keep her footing on the wet and weedy shelves where the snow had melted, and she was well aware that all the attention of the man on top (or coming down the steps) would be concentrated in his hearing. The shelves seemed endless and she thought she must have passed the foot of her conjectured upward traverse; it was almost impossible to tell in the poor visibility whether a slanting break was continuous or merely a blind start that led nowhere. An easy climb she might follow silently; but if she had to retreat down rock that was above her standard she might fall and that would be an end of caution, and probably the end of her.

She tried to remember the image of the cliff as she had seen it this morning; was there nothing, no distinguishing feature that marked the start of this possible escape route? There had been some vague qualification in her mind: it was a pretty climb but. . . . But what? Why should *she* qualify her opinion? Because the line was broken, like the ledge in Ogof Lladron, or the rock looked loose, or greasy? In none of those instances would she have thought it pretty. She was middle-aged and she could stand to lose some weight; she had excellent balance (that goes last) but she was no longer supple; gymnastic feats were beyond her, and so were overhangs. Overhangs. That was it: at the lower end of the climb the cliff was undercut.

Looking for the place she felt trapped. He has given up waiting now, she thought; he has come down the staircase and is moving along the ledges. She listened but the sea was rising and would have drowned the sound even of nailed boots. It occurred to her that if the fog didn't clear and if he didn't know of this escape route, if it were an escape, she might elude him yet, providing he wasn't waiting at the top.

Suddenly she saw the start of what could be the ledge: if she could reach it. The overhang was a tall, shallow depression like a monstrous coffin with one good hold high up on the edge of its left wall.

There were incipient bulges on either side of the depression which just held her feet as she straddled upwards. There was very little for the hands until she could reach that hold on the left. Underneath it and outside on the face of the rock there were one or two small footholds. She had no guarantee that the route would continue above; that it was the start of her fine ascending line she had no doubt but there are two kinds of line in this context: the climber's which is a passage, however hard, and the artist's which need be only a shadow on the rock. Once committed there could be no going back; it was up with a swing and a heave, and she was twenty feet or so above the ground. A fall at her age would mean a broken leg at best.

The handhold was hard and jagged. Her hand curled over it with an old familiarity. She was leaning left and her right foot was coming off. She brought her right hand over to the crucial hold and swung sideways. In a fine surge of muscle and youthful memory she stepped up the wall, pressed down on her hands and mantelshelfed on a hold as big as a dinner plate.

Leftwards and up ran a big red crack; the snow had melted here and the rock was wet but rough and, if it was steeper than it had appeared from a distance, it was as solid as granite. Other cracks ran parallel above; there was an embarrassment of holds. In her joy at discovering a classic route she almost forgot why she was there. She started to move: gently, quietly, but as the sound of the sea receded, she listened for signs from above: something to tell her that the killer was waiting, but there was no sign.

Once as she climbed she felt an airy break in the atmosphere and, looking up, saw blue sky and, horrible in its visibility, the brown edge of the cliff about fifty feet above. The snow had stopped. She froze on her holds and one leg started to shake. At any moment the fog would roll away and, wherever he was, he would see her crucified on the wall, and there would come that sound like gas popping in a doll's house. She wondered if he were a good marksman. She would prefer to be dead when she fell.

The break closed and the fog was thicker than ever. She went on, finding snow in the crack now, and having to clear each hold with her hands before she could use it. Suddenly she was at the top and she stepped out on snow-covered turf that was broken by rocks and drifted clumps of dead thrift. The hotel must be over on her left.

The continued silence was uncanny. Perhaps he had gone away, but she had heard no sound of a vehicle. She had been attended by such good luck so far that she daren't push it farther. She decided to avoid the hotel and her car and, keeping parallel with the track but well away from it, she would hope the fog remained long enough for her to reach the main road. At least now she had the benefit of the gorse if she needed concealment.

To avoid the road she had to find it first and was startled to come on it after only a few steps. There were the tracks of one vehicle. She couldn't tell which way they were going so if the driver had come to the Schooner after the snow fell, he was still there. They were broader than car tracks. She started to walk quickly inland and almost immediately she heard an engine behind her.

There was a long low rock a few yards from the road. She ran and threw herself behind it and tore off her red balaclava.

It passed slowly, without lights. It was a strange Land Rover with a Merioneth registration: FFF. The Centre's vehicle was LJC.

Chapter Fourteen

THE SNOW WAS dangerous; not that it had started to fall again but she left tracks. It would be too easy to find her if someone were still searching. Even the driver of the Land Rover must have seen her prints if he'd glanced away from the road. She returned to the hotel warily, looking for signs that might show it was occupied.

The building loomed through the fog. There were no lights so far as she could see and her car stood by the front door where she had left it. There was no other vehicle on the forecourt and the only tracks were those of the Land Rover. It had been parked beside her car.

She opened the front door with Dawson's key and turned right at the end of the main passage where he had said she would find his sitting room.

It was a bright chintzy place but she didn't spend time studying it for the focus of attention was an open window with a broken pane.

The telephone stood on an occasional table. She lifted the receiver and dialled 999, her glance travelling round the room and coming back to the doorway. Then she realised that the line was dead. The severed ends of the flex dangled against the skirting board.

She shut the front door behind her and went to her car. The door wasn't locked—but she had locked it. She switched on the ignition and the starter whirred hopelessly.

Certain now that there was no need for caution she hurried round to the outbuildings where she found an old van in an open shed and, beyond, a garage with double doors which should have been bolted and padlocked, but now the padlock was forced and the doors hung open. The Sunbeam inside was unlocked. There were no keys in either the van or the car.

She let herself into the house again, searched quickly and superficially through an upstairs bedroom and the sitting room, then left for the main road on foot, comforting herself with the thought that although a car would have provided speed and a spurious sense of safety, she would be less conspicuous walking.

She hadn't reckoned with the weather, for after she had been on the slushy road for about twenty minutes, the fog started to clear.

She looked round quickly to get her bearings and saw cloud banks in all directions but these were evaporating like smoke before the rising wind. She was only about a hundred yards from the point where the Porth Bach track came in, and about two miles from the main road.

The track from the Schooner lay along the crest of the moor and she felt very vulnerable. No Land Rover nor any other vehicle was visible and for all she could see of people she might have been the only person between the main road and the cliffs, but she didn't know that both Land Rover and driver might not be concealed behind a clump of gorse waiting for her to come within range.

She looked along the line of the Porth Bach track but saw no vehicle although there could have been one in a dip. The Adams' whitewashed cottage showed up well and she thought she caught a glimpse of Dawson's launch beyond the jetty but otherwise the sea, like the road, was empty.

In order to get off the sky-line she dropped down to the left where the moorland sloped to the western cliffs of the headland. The ground changed here from turf and gorse to thick snow-covered heather. There were no paths and no houses, and the absence of life gave such an eerie aspect to this desolate tract that she was grateful to see the grey backs of sheep; they represented a return to normality.

The light was fading by the time she reached the main road and started walking west. She wouldn't go east; for all she knew

169

the man with the gun would be waiting for her at the end of the Schooner track.

She stopped the first vehicle that came along. It was a laundry van and, telling the driver that her car had broken down, she asked him to take her to the nearest telephone kiosk. This turned out to be in the village of Glanaber and when the van driver had put her down, she saw a police house across the road with a green Mini in the drive.

The officer was fat and ponderous and it was obvious that the last thing he wanted was business just as he was looking forward to his tea and the evening's television. Miss Pink felt sorry for him because he didn't look like a man who would enjoy anything other than vicarious excitement even when he was committed.

No, he said, she could not use his telephone to speak to Superintendent Pryce but if she would tell him, Constable Edwards, what the trouble was, he would see that the superintendent received the message. There was an implicit suggestion that P.C. Edwards would be the judge of its importance and perhaps even of its being sent at all.

She hesitated, calculating, then she asked for pencil and paper and as she talked she wrote a list of numbered items. *1.* (she wrote) *Mrs Wolkoff.* The superintendent was to be told that her body was in Ogof Lladron and that she had been stabbed. *2. The Murderer?* An armed man had driven an old Land Rover with the registration FFF away from the Schooner, after failing to shoot Miss Pink. *3. Schooner.* The telephone line had been cut and Mr Dawson was somewhere between Porth Bach and the main road on foot.

She gave him the paper and he started to read, his lips moving. She went out, crossed to the telephone kiosk and got through to police headquarters. Pryce was not available, she was told; she should try the police station at Bontddu.

She rang the Goat and Olwen answered. Mr Roberts wasn't in; he was at Plas Mawr. Miss Pink thanked her and, after making sure that Pryce wasn't at the hotel, she rang off before the woman could question her.

She dialled the Centre's number and Sally answered. Ted had just left to go to the Goat.

'Right,' Miss Pink said, 'what's happening with you—quickly? Are the boys all right?'

They weren't. Two were missing and had not been seen since midday when they had become separated from the other members of their party in the blizzard. At that time they had been approaching the top of the high and extensive face called Craig yr Adar but the visibility had been so bad that the surviving boys said that they had seen no sign of the cliff. Another group, following the leadership of a boy with more sense, had come down from the ridge and passed underneath the cliff. Shouts had been heard soon after midday from somewhere around the middle of it.

'And that's where they're concentrating,' Sally said, 'along the foot of the face and up the gullies, but conditions are so atrocious that Rowland says it would be hopeless trying to look for anyone on top; you can't stand on the ridge. The wind is gale force and there's about six inches of new snow and it's drifting.'

'Is Lithgow in charge of the rescue?'

'He's vanished. He hasn't been seen since eight o'clock this morning when he checked his patrol out of camp—except by the police who spoke to him for a moment but the weather was getting worse very quickly and he told them that he was going to call off the high-level route and get the parties down to the valley. He left to intercept the boys and that's the last the police saw of him. None of the boys have seen him either. And that's why they were all on the top today: because he didn't reach them to tell them to come down.'

'I wondered,' Miss Pink said. 'Was he in the Centre's Land Rover?'

'Yes. They've not found that either. The police have been looking for it.'

'All the other instructors are out, I suppose?'

'They must be searching for the boys. The R.A.F. team's out as well. Linda and I are holding the fort here, seeing the lads into hot baths and dry clothes as they come in, and we'll make sure they're fed, don't worry.'

Miss Pink tried the Goat again and Ted came on the line. He was full of Lithgow and she was about to interrupt when she realised he was telling her that the Centre's Land Rover had been found—on the camp site below the ramp that led to the mine entrance: 'They're in the mines now. They think he might be reckoning on some grand gesture, like blowing up the lot—'

'Can you get hold of Pryce?' she interrupted.

'I wouldn't try. He's torn in two. The more men he can put in the mines, the more likely he is to flush Lithgow before he succeeds—and the more lives he'll lose if the lot goes up.'

'Lithgow isn't in the mine,' she said, talking slowly and firmly: 'The Land Rover is a red herring, so was sending the boys on the high-level route. He's desperate to keep people away from Porth Bach. The explosives Lithgow's interested in are in the Adams' cottage, not in the mine. Lithgow's down here; he tried to kill me.'

She told him about the second murder and the shot fired at her below the Schooner: 'He stole the second Land Rover to replace his own after he abandoned that in a place where it would put you all off the scent. Something's planned for tonight; everything points to it. If you can't get Pryce on the phone, tell them to get him on a radio. But you shouldn't leave the hotel. Stay near the phone.'

'They'll take a devil of a lot of convincing—'

'That's your job,' she snapped, 'but Mrs Wolkoff was killed down here and so was Bett Martin. Lithgow's not blowing himself up in the mine, he's going to try to save what's at Porth Bach. If you get time to ring the Coastguard I think you'll find that a converted torpedo boat is making for here too.'

It was after six o'clock and she was driving slowly eastwards on the main road and nearing the turn to Bethel when a police car passed at high speed going in the opposite direction. She turned and followed. So P.C. Edwards had thought the message worthy of instant transmission after all.

The distance between the two vehicles increased. Miss Pink's was an ancient Commer van which she had hired from the Glanaber butcher for five pounds—a price which, she reflected grimly, was probably its market value as scrap.

She passed the lay-by where the track crossed the fields to Porth Bach. It was deserted, and so was a telephone kiosk some few hundred yards to the west. She made a mental note of that for future reference. Half a mile ahead she saw the police car turn on the Schooner track. With this kind of protection the dark country lost its forbidding aspect and became merely background again. Then she remembered. With stakes like a cottage full of explosives they'd be prepared to take very high risks, or would the risks have been anticipated and very carefully calculated?

She turned left again and realised that she had lost the police. Surely they hadn't gone to the Schooner? She drove carefully with her headlights full on, then she topped a gentle rise and saw tail lights some distance ahead. There was a considerable wind down here and pieces of rubbish and dead stalks were hurled against the windscreen.

She passed the place where Charles had slept in her Austin, the point where the Jaguar left the road, and then, approaching the next passing-place, above Puffin Cove, she saw that she was overhauling the police car. She slowed down and realised that it was stationary.

It had stopped with its doors open and the interior light on, and its headlights trained on the green Mini which she had last seen in the Glanaber constable's drive. Now it was slewed across the road with its door wedged open by his body, the head towards her and the eyes open. In her own lights she saw the detective, Williams, crouched behind the big police car. He was staring over his shoulder at her and his face held the curiously blank expression, without fear or hope, of a man expecting death. She had seen that expression in the mountains and, as she identified it, realised that she was the cause. Williams didn't know who was in the Commer.

She switched off her lights and gradually, as her eyes became accustomed to that curious stage scene ahead: the side of the green Mini with the word POLICE on it, the tumbled body, and a small odd shape that was Williams' feet silhouetted against the reflected light, she distinguished movement on the right of the police car, and she assumed that Pryce was there, perhaps with others.

Gusts of wind shook her van and, picking gravel from the road, flung it like hail against the metal. Almost subconsciously she wondered how the wind could raise gravel from under the slush.

There was a flash on the left of the road and the sound of a shot was followed by others, louder and heavier. With the windows closed against the wild fluctuations of the wind, the noise of gunfire was confused and all sense of direction was lost. Then the fusillade stopped and there was no movement on the offside of the police car. When the next shots came the participants seemed to have shifted to the right and she could see no feet against the light. What she did see was a fast-running form which came from the left to toss something in the car ahead and retreated so quickly it might have been an illusion except that now the car's interior was a riot of flames which streamed back towards her in the teeth of the gale.

She started her engine and by the light of the offside indicator reversed with her head out of the opened window, fully aware that only a few yards below the unfenced tarmac the cliffs dropped into Puffin Cove. The air was full of spray.

A bullet crashed against some metal part of the van. She withdrew her head and turned her neck painfully, grateful that she could turn it at all. She switched on her headlights and saw that she hadn't reversed far enough. She put out the lights and continued backwards, hearing the crash and roar of the sea below the wind.

This time, when she switched on, the passing-place was in front. She turned carefully (recalling the Jaguar with horror) but as fast as she could force the worn gears to mesh. Then she put her foot down and, except for the two turns, didn't lift it until she reached the telephone kiosk on the main road.

Ted had taken her at her word and remained at the Goat. She told him what was happening on the cliffs, that one police radio would have been put out of action and the other was now in flames, and she emphasised the need for speed in sending reinforcements. As she stopped talking, he said quickly: 'You were right about the torpedo boat!' and cut the connection.

She put down the receiver and thought that this was the end for her; there was nothing else she could do. She pushed open the door of the kiosk and stood in the blustery night thinking that she was at last safe from gunfire: everyone else was engaged elsewhere. Time was working on two planes: she had reached the anti-climax but the others were still concerned with the crescendo. She wondered where Dawson was.

She looked towards the coast but she remembered that even in daylight the cliffs and cove would be hidden by slightly rising ground, although she fancied she could see a flickering light which might be the burning car.

She could never do nothing in an emergency and now she started to stroll towards the stile where the footpath began. After a few steps she checked, turned back to the van and, taking the torch from her rucksack, adjusted it on her head.

The snowy fields were windswept and untenanted, for even the cows were in the barns. An occasional light showed in a farm but the night was too noisy for the dogs to hear her and none barked. There was no moon but above the coast the sky was clear and the combination of stars and snow resulted in a weak light against which she could see the tops of walls and the first of the battered thorns as she approached the ravine. She didn't use her light.

The wind was raging in the tops of the trees but as she climbed down from the last stile she couldn't fail to hear a report and a vicious crack as, for the second time that day, she heard a bullet strike rock. She stood quite still and, in a lull in the wind, called to the darkness ahead:

'I haven't got a gun.'

The first trees were black before her where they stepped down the slope but as she stared, part of the blackness detached itself and moved forward across the snow: a figure that carried something which could only be a rifle. The person, shorter and slighter than Miss Pink, stood beside her and a few feet away.

'Move down into the trees,' Nell Harvey said.

Chapter Fifteen

'I can't see your face,' Miss Pink said stupidly.

'It's a black stocking.'

When they came to the wood the girl stopped the older woman at the first trees and herself moved a few steps farther. Thus she had the stile and Miss Pink almost in line. It was sheltered here and there was no sound but the low rush of wind and the creak of branches. Miss Pink turned towards the other and stared with fascination at the black void where a face should be.

'Why did you miss twice?' she asked.

'I didn't aim at you here—and it was Slade on the cliff.'

'*Slade?*' She absorbed this, then she asked ironically: 'Wasn't he aiming at me either?'

'He meant to kill you but he isn't a good marksman. No one else was available at the time.'

'Why should he shoot to kill, but not you?'

'He was meant to stop you getting help. We'd worked hard enough to keep the police in the mountains.'

'How did you know we'd found the body?'

'He's been down here since soon after ten this morning. If it hadn't been for the snowstorm he would have shot you both as you left Ogof Lladron. Then he thought he'd get you as you came up to the hotel and never guessed that Dawson would go back to Porth Bach and leave you to come ashore alone.'

'So he did realise I was alone?'

'Eventually, but he's slow. Then, when he thought he'd killed you, he realised Dawson had put back to Porth Bach so he went there.'

'Did he kill Dawson?'

'No, he was too late there as well.' Her voice was expressionless and Miss Pink asked curiously:

'Why do you—use him?'

There was a long pause and she thought the girl was not going to answer. Perhaps she was considering Slade's intrinsic worth, for at last she said:

'He does what he's told without question...which isn't enough. Sometimes they have to act on their own initiative. Lithgow is better.' Then she asked with a hint of interest: 'How did you get out of that place?'

Miss Pink told her about the syncline.

'That's what I told Slade,' the girl remarked, 'but he said that if you weren't dead, you were injured, and anyway you were too old. Lithgow wouldn't have made that mistake.'

'How did Slade get to the hotel?'

'Yes, transport has been difficult. It had to be left to chance but I was banking on someone being careless, and they were. Slade stole a truck first thing this morning while a farmer was getting his sheep down.'

'And while he was stalking us along the cliffs, I suppose you and Lithgow were setting up that search operation?'

'Not much setting up to do. Once the boys had been sent on the tops in that weather, trouble followed naturally.'

'Were you on top at all?'

'Oh yes. Lithgow and I were up there muddling things as much as we could—until it was time to leave. Then we met at the camp site and I brought him down here in the Mini.'

The girl made a sudden gesture and Miss Pink flinched. She caught sight of a tiny glow. The other was looking at her watch.

'Was it you in the mine?' Miss Pink asked.

'Yes.'

'Were you trying to kill us?'

'No, just watching. If I'd shot you your bodies would have floated in the loom and I didn't want to attract attention until we'd got the explosives away from the cove.'

'But you were doing field-work with the boys while we were in the mine.'

'The boys were on field-work. No one asked me where I was for an hour or so.'

'Slade confused me,' Miss Pink said conversationally. 'He was on the defensive when we met him on the estuary. I wondered at the time if it was him in the mine. What *was* he hiding?'

'At the estuary?'

'When the last canoe expedition was coming in.'

'Of course. I sent him to warn Lithgow that they'd discovered the break-in at the mine. He was waiting for Lithgow when you arrived, using a puncture as an excuse to stay there. He could cope with Wright but after you came, he wouldn't get a chance to speak to Lithgow privately, so he left. As it happened Lithgow had seen the Mini from the sea and was careful what he said when he came in.'

The girl moved again and Miss Pink felt that time was getting short but she wanted an answer to her original question.

'Why didn't *you* kill me?' she asked.

'It wasn't necessary.'

'You mean I'm no longer dangerous?'

'Not to us.' Was there a hint of amusement in the cool voice?

'It's nearly time to go,' Nell said.

'You don't kill when it's unnecessary then?' Miss Pink pressed.

'No. Why should we? We're not wanton.'

' " Wanton",' Miss Pink repeated. 'How are these explosives to be used?'

'Not wantonly. They're much too valuable. They'll be used very selectively—and only after careful discussion—where they'll cause the most damage.'

'To morale?'

'Possibly.'

'In tower blocks of flats, for instance?'

There was a sharp movement in the gloom but when the girl spoke again she sounded tired.

'There are innocent people—and children—being repressed and starved and tortured, systematically, everywhere. Are you worried about *them*? Don't be a hypocrite, Miss Pink.'

'I thought you didn't care about world problems. You seemed so objective about them.'

'Problems,' the girl repeated thoughtfully. 'Yes, I gave up

"problems" some time ago. They become unbearable, and you go mad—or kill yourself, like Cary Paterson.'

' "A weak character", you said.'

'Yes; if it's so bad that you feel a compulsion to take your own life, why not channel that energy outwards, towards the people who are making the problems?'

'Capitalists?'

'No, Miss Pink, don't make me out a Communist; they're part of the established order too.'

'Are you anarchists?'

'No. We put our faith in a strong government.'

'I see. You're going to overthrow the world order so that you can set up another in its place. What will be different about it?'

'This one will be better.'

'Founded on violence and the lives of innocent people. What's the difference between killing babies in Vietnam and killing them in Ireland?'

'You're bringing sentiment into it.'

'My God!' Miss Pink exclaimed, and Nell said hurriedly:

'Hypocrisy, I mean. We're honest.'

'I wonder why you're doing this,' Miss Pink murmured in all sincerity, 'what the basic motive is.'

'We have to survive—any way.'

'Why can't you do it politically?'

'We'd never get the votes.'

'It's Fascism. You know that, don't you?'

There was no reply. A branch cracked in the ravine, or it could have been a distant shot.

'Time to go,' Nell said, 'you first. Don't use your light or they'll shoot at it.'

It wasn't hard to see under the trees, for the path was a white trail. They came to Mrs Wolkoff's cottage and, at that moment, heard more shots ahead.

They stopped and in the ensuing silence Miss Pink whispered:

'It was you in the woods that morning. You saw me with her.'

'Yes.'

'Did you kill her?'

'Yes.'

'How did you get her body to the cave?'

The silence stretched and Miss Pink realised that she was alone. She continued down the path. There was an intermittent popping of gunfire from the cliffs.

She slipped inside the old barn beyond Miss Lupin's place and looked down to the shore. Lights were bobbing back and forth between the Adams' cottage and the jetty. She wondered how far the loading had progressed. Cottage and jetty were dark and since she had been working by starlight for what seemed a very long time she was shocked when a sudden glare of light erupted from high on the western rim of the cove and moved, lowering its trajectory to sweep the jetty, the torpedo boat moored alongside, and scurrying figures, then, still moving, the light swung towards her, passed, and she saw headlights descending the road. As other vehicles followed, the jetty was lit and plunged into darkness alternately until one set of lights stayed trained on the scene where the pale decks of the boat gleamed in the light but all the people had vanished.

Gunfire started again and the leading car stopped. All the lights went out except those of the stationary vehicle on top. Miss Pink could hear men shouting. Up on the cliff the headlights burned implacably and nothing moved on the jetty or the boat. Then from the east side of the cove a rifle spoke methodically. The lights went out and the cove was in darkness again.

Someone dropped a heavy iron object on stone. It could have been a signal, for soon afterwards she became aware of deep throbbing from the direction of the jetty. The gunfire petered out and there was a lot of shouting from the road.

Engines exploded to roaring life and again the cove was floodlit by an approaching car to show the sleek black boat starting to move away from the jetty towards the open sea.

The lights wheeled and there were men running down from the elbow, slowing to a walk, staring seaward.

Miss Pink left the barn and had just reached the turning-circle when a deep boom sounded beyond the mouth of the cove.

There were exclamations from a group of people on the jetty. Out to sea a cold white beam wavered across the tossing water, slipped over something, returned and fastened on the fleeing boat.

'What's that with the searchlight?' asked an authoritative voice, 'Coastguard?'

'It's a patrol boat.' With astonishment and relief Miss Pink recognised Dawson's breathless voice.

'How the hell did it get here?' This could be the chief constable.

'I sent for it,' Dawson explained, 'the captain's a friend of mine.'

'Where from?' Miss Pink asked, meaning the patrol boat.

'That's Miss Pink!' exclaimed Pryce.

'From Mrs Wolkoff's cottage,' Dawson said.

'They're going to get away!' someone shouted.

'But she can't be faster than a patrol boat!' Dawson protested.

A voice said: 'If they're running that torpedo job on the old engines she can do forty knots.'

'Hasn't our chap any firing power?' asked the chief constable.

'He's got a forty-millimetre, sir,' Pryce said, 'but I don't think he'll dare use it—except—'

Following the line of the searchlight beam but a little below it, a bright spark moved surprisingly slowly towards the torpedo boat.

'Tracer,' someone said, and at that moment a huge silent sunburst of flame bloomed in the bay—then the roar of the explosion hit them and they threw themselves on the ground.

Lying there, peering along the stones, then lifting their heads to look over the crumbling parapet, they saw, no longer a boat but a few odd pieces of burning debris on the sea, pale in the searchlight's glare.

'That's the end of that,' Pryce said with a kind of quiet awe, standing up carefully. Miss Pink made her way towards his voice. Torches were being shone.

'Were they all on the boat?' she asked.

'No, neither of them. Lithgow's dead and we've got Slade alive. They were the marksmen on the cliff. Blew up the road first and shot a constable before we got there.'

'I know,' she said, 'but Nell Harvey was on the boat.'

'Nell Harvey? What's she got to do with it?'

'Everything,' Miss Pink said.

Chapter Sixteen

'I t's the duplicity that I can't accept,' Sir Thomas said, 'here she was entrusted with the training of youth; we believed her competent, diligent—' he paused, at a loss. 'Wholesome?' suggested Beresford.

'And all the time,' Sir Thomas continued, ignoring him, 'for two years, she had been plotting, stealing.... Stealing from Global! In effect, from her employers; from *us!*'

It was a week after the gun battle at Porth Bach and the directors were again assembled in the library at Plas Mawr. It was Friday evening and the police cadets were attending a film show under the supervision of the duty instructor, Rowland Hughes.

After the strain of that gruelling search operation (with the missing boys found alive and safe, but miles from Craig yr Adar), after being deprived of three of its staff at one blow, and without a warden, the Centre was struggling on with Sally and Miss Pink in the office, and Ted, Hughes and Wright running the outdoor activities with the help of a man loaned by Outward Bound. Linda, pale and subdued, had stayed on as matron at her own insistence. Afterwards, she said, she might return to Birmingham.

'I could understand it better if the girl had gone in for demonstrating,' Sir Thomas protested, 'or sit-ins, perhaps—but this meticulous subversion over a period of time: it's inhuman.'

'She was mad,' Beresford said flatly.

Miss Pink and Ted had compiled a report. The police had discovered something of the past history of the three instructors, not much, but Slade had filled in a lot of gaps concerning recent events. When he'd learned that Nell had confessed to the murder of Mrs Wolkoff, he talked, for no other reason, it seemed, than to express his feeling for the girl. He adored her.

Beresford had interrupted Miss Pink there.

'Ha! So they were lovers.'

'No.'

'What? It was Lithgow then?'

'I don't know.' Miss Pink was puzzled. 'It's irrelevant anyway. Why do you harp on it?'

'Well, that's how it all started: with Lithgow telling Linda he was having an affair with Nell. No, it was Bett first—'

'That was complete fabrication. As Ted said, they had no time for affairs, although it wasn't climbing that occupied their minds. Lithgow claimed an affair with Bett only in order to justify those evenings away from home. In fact, his mind was so far divorced from sex that I expect he'd never anticipated Linda suddenly breaking down and demanding to know where he spent his evenings. He was thrown off-balance and quickly thought of Bett, who was the obvious choice, without realising the danger. When he did, or when Nell pointed it out to him, he substituted Nell.'

'Then Linda must have guessed the truth as soon as Bett's body was found.'

'I doubt it,' Miss Pink said comfortably. 'In any case,' she added as she saw Beresford wanted to follow that line, 'Lithgow didn't kill Bett.'

'Then who—?'

'It would be better to go back to the beginning,' Ted said gently.

Miss Pink looked to see if she had Sir Thomas' attention, then she referred to the report in front of her:

'Nell Harvey was a member of a militant group until about two and a half years ago. The police can find no trace of her between then and when she turned up here six months later. Slade won't talk about it, on the other hand he is insistent on her proficiency as a marksman so I think we can take it that she was trained as a terrorist during that time. Where, is a matter for conjecture.

'She took this post with us and Lithgow followed, then Slade. They made no secret about knowing each other; they didn't need to: their climbing was an excellent cover. Lithgow was the explosives expert; he was probably trained when Linda thought he was in the Alps for six months. Nell was the leader of the cell, the organiser. Slade was the strong-arm man. He carried out orders. Those are his words. He doesn't mean them as justification for what he did, they're a fact.'

'So *he* killed Bett,' Beresford said, but Miss Pink was going to tell the story in her own way.

'I worked backwards from the leg of lamb,' she told them, looking up from the report, 'that was when my ideas started to crystallise, when I felt that something had happened to Mrs Wolkoff. I wondered if Bett turned the Jaguar in the cove after all, and Mrs Wolkoff saw her there.

'At the place on the cliffs where the Jaguar had been parked I tried to identify with Bett's state of mind, sitting there with the engine running and waiting for Hughes. She was drunk and annoyed and probably thinking of leaving him to walk home anyway. She might have been about to drive on to turn round in Porth Bach—when a vehicle passed. Now suppose she was parked so that the Jaguar was concealed from anything approaching from the west but in such a position that she could see the other vehicle and its rear number plate as it went by. Recognising the Land Rover, knowing that Lithgow took it home, she would follow, perhaps to find out what he was up to, or simply thinking that here was a fresh companion who would be more fun than Hughes in his present state.

'According to Slade this is pretty well what happened except that there was more than one of them. The Mini, with Slade and Nell, always followed the loaded Land Rover, ready for emergencies. Nell drove with side lights on the cliff and when Bett pulled out to follow the Land Rover, she was trapped— although she wouldn't know that. Lithgow had Davigdor with him that night and they realised immediately that there was another car between them and the Mini but they weren't too worried because, although it was an odd time to be there, the

Centre had a legitimate excuse to be in the cove and, besides, there were Nell and Slade behind. So the Land Rover drove to the turning-circle followed by the two cars and when they stopped, Nell went to the Jaguar and asked Bett how she came to be alone.

'Bett told her about Hughes; she suspected nothing—there was no reason why she should suspect anything criminal even if she were sober—and in her state of mind the prospect of a drinking party was irresistible. She went inside the cottage with them and Slade strangled her. Then, leaving Davigdor and Lithgow to unload the explosives, the other two returned to the cliff in the Mini and the Jaguar.

'Before disposing of the body and the car they looked for Hughes and found him, but when Nell saw that he was dead drunk, she left him. One would like to think that she spared him because, as she told me, they didn't kill unnecessarily, but that wasn't the case. Nell hoped the Jaguar would be submerged at low tide but she couldn't depend on it. If the murder came to light, Hughes was to be the fall-guy.

'Nell was prudent. Having disposed of the body, she collected the others, dropped Davigdor near Bethel (she wanted no tie-up with him) and rushed the gang to Bontddu in order to establish an alibi for all of them in case it should be needed at any time.'

'She was also prudent about the canoes,' Ted put in.

'Ah yes. She planned meticulously but she was also a superb opportunist. By normal standards our canoes went too far west, as the Coastguard pointed out. This was necessary to Nell so that the activity justified the Centre's vehicles being at Porth Bach so often and at odd times. As with the Army, people have got used to adventure schools and their curious operations. Of course, all those vehicles in the cove on the night of the murder left tracks and this explains the reasoning behind that unseasonal canoe trip which was laid on at the last moment, the purpose of which was to cover or confuse the tracks the Land Rover and Mini had left on Saturday, but above all to erase those made by the Jaguar. Nell didn't want it known that Bett had been to the cove. It might focus attention too close to the Adams' cottage.'

'But Mrs Wolkoff saw them—is that it?' Sir Thomas eyed her askance.

'Yes,' Miss Pink said, 'she was a rather monstrous old lady but she didn't deserve—that. I doubt if she had any idea of the gang's true activities although Nell was certainly using her, perhaps even implying that she was engaged on similar work, but secret. She'd certainly get the old lady's co-operation that way. She kept Nell informed of everything that happened in the cove but she must have become too curious. Perhaps she was in Miss Lupin's barn and saw Bett go in the Adams' cottage, or she went down in daylight and found the imprint of the Jaguar on the turning-circle—at all events, Nell saw me with Mrs Wolkoff on Wednesday morning, when the girl was keeping an eye on the cove on her day off, and she couldn't risk the old lady talking.

'Mrs Wolkoff was killed after I left Porth Bach, and her body was inside the cottage when Pryce telephoned. Nell typed the letter to the postman, of course. The post mortem findings were that Mrs Wolkoff was stabbed, neatly, through the ribs. It must have been done in the open. There was very little blood but Nell wouldn't have taken the risk of doing it indoors.

'That evening, after the party in the Goat, Slade and Nell went to Porth Bach by way of the fields because the police car was still stationed on the cliffs, and they rowed the body to Ogof Lladron.'

'They were running a fearful risk,' Beresford interposed, 'with the police car on top.'

Miss Pink shook her head.

'They had reconnoitred the cliffs on foot and they were both well-trained. Neither would make a noise. Slade says the police were smoking in the car with the windows closed and would have heard nothing. They were, after all, under orders to stop anything approaching Porth Bach on the road. They couldn't be expected to watch the sea and the cliffs—and Ogof Lladron was over a mile away. With muffled oars and no lights, they were fairly secure.'

'Going back a bit,' Beresford said, 'I had a feeling of trouble before I left for the States—not *this* kind of trouble,' he added hastily as Miss Pink and Ted looked at him with stony eyes, 'but once murder had been committed, what focused attention on the Centre? I mean, surely almost anyone could have killed Bett?'

Ted frowned, thinking back.

'First,' he said slowly, 'they suspected Martín, which is virtually a traditional reaction—'

'It was the lighter,' Miss Pink put in, 'Mrs Wolkoff would phone Nell to say she'd seen the Jaguar in the sea. So, by way of extra insurance, Nell picked up the lighter on Monday morning at breakfast. Slade planted it on the cliffs Tuesday evening after the report of the post mortem came through. That lighter was Nell's mistake. Once Hughes was eliminated as a suspect, or rather, when he seemed an unlikely murderer, suspicion still stayed at the Centre because the staff had so many more opportunities of stealing the lighter than someone from outside.'

'I see,' Beresford said with an air of relief, 'I find it rather comforting that the girl should make a mistake.'

'It needn't have been fatal,' Miss Pink pointed out, 'She was only playing for time. Things had got too hot for them and this was the last load they'd get from the area. Nell guessed that on Saturday morning when she saw the activity at the mine. They would have planned to escape themselves on the torpedo boat's next trip. Nell almost did it, you know. She would have got away if it hadn't been for Dawson.'

'He's the man, apart from Miss Pink, who wins my admiration,' Ted said, laughing. 'He showed a most judicious blend of courage and caution.'

Miss Pink smiled.

'I thought he didn't hear my shout and the rockfall,' she told them, 'but he'd heard, and although he hadn't guessed the truth but had put the worst construction on the sounds, he decided that the anchorage wasn't a healthy place, and since I'd told him to look out for himself, he did just that and made all speed to Porth Bach, ripped up his jersey, wrapped the rags round his oars and rowed ashore well east of the beach. He was contouring the cove when the fog cleared and from above Mrs

Wolkoff's place he saw a dinghy leaving his launch. He was too far away to see who it was but, in fact, this was Slade who, as Nell said, arrived too late.

'Dawson lay low and saw Slade go in the Adams' cottage. He wanted to stay and watch developments but he also needed to contact the police about what he thought were two murders: mine and Mrs Wolkoff's. He compromised by going down to the cottage and entering as we did by the broken window and telephoning from there.

'He couldn't find Pryce but he did eventually get on to an inspector at Bontddu who was a friend and who told him that I'd phoned through from Glanaber asking for all possible reinforcements at Porth Bach. Then this man made what was, to Dawson, the startling revelation that Ted had come through with a story about the Adams' cottage being full of explosives.

'After he'd put down the receiver he was still in the bedroom when he saw Nell go up the ravine carrying a rifle. He didn't know it was Nell because it was getting dark; all he could distinguish was a figure with a gun. Guessing that a guard was being put on the cove, he started to make his way seaward, going uphill at first to use the trees as cover. Then he saw activity on the water and could just make out a biggish boat coming in. That was when he guessed the explosives were going out that night and suddenly realised that the action was tailor-made for his friend in Holyhead harbour. The Royal Navy boat was keeping a weather eye open for illicit traffic during the Irish emergency.

'Dawson rushed back and telephoned this gentleman, who jumped at the chance of activity. Then he worked his way up through the trees again until he had a partial view of the cove, but now it was almost dark and he had to go a long way seaward in order to see anything. It was while he was doing this that he saw an explosion on the cliff top. That was Lithgow blowing up the road. Dawson thought it must be some kind of ambush so back he went to the cottage to report but this time the telephone was dead. Nell must have done that; the wires were severed at the top of the wood.'

Miss Pink stopped talking and there was silence broken at length by Sir Thomas: 'Who killed young Edwards from Glanaber?'

'Lithgow.'

'So each of them got someone in the end,' Beresford remarked absently.

'They got far more than that,' Miss Pink corrected him sternly, 'they had been running the stuff across to Ireland for well over a year. They must have been responsible for many, many deaths.'

Beresford coughed.

'There was no way of knowing—'

'Of course not,' she assured him, 'the whole operation was very carefully planned and the operators hand-picked. Davigdor was another who was selected for the job. He was the lessee of the cottage but his references were impeccable. There is a curious mixture of evil and conformity here. The Adams are completely in the clear, by the way, and Davigdor's references were genuine, as was his underwater exploration, like the alpine routes he and the others had done. It's fascinating how innocent activities were dovetailed with the criminal.

'It was Davigdor who stole the lorries from the Army depot, for the sole purpose of creating a diversion. It didn't need much: only a handful of men, a little paint and false number plates. In view of those lorries and the implication that they were used in the theft, the police concentrated on areas hundreds of miles away, while all the time the haul was waiting at Porth Bach to be shipped out.

'Davigdor's job originally was to clear the harbour for the torpedo boat then, in order not to excite suspicion, he and his divers had to pretend to continue underwater activities, which in turn attracted a genuine club. However, the more activity there was in the bay of an innocent order, the better cover was provided for, the illegal traffic, and the importance of that was demonstrated on that last day when the Coastguard actually logged the torpedo boat round the coast but took no special interest because they were so used to seeing her in the area.'

'What will Slade get?' Beresford asked after a pause.

'Life, of course,' Ted told him. 'He admitted killing Bett when he was told that Nell had confessed to Mrs Wolkoff's murder. He also wounded Williams. Fortunately, as Nell said, he wasn't a good marksman.'

'But what about the others?' Sir Thomas asked, 'the men behind the scenes, the ones at the top?'

No one answered him.

'But I mean to say,' he protested, staring round the table, 'someone was behind it, weren't they? Someone directed them. Hasn't Slade talked?'

'Not about that,' Ted said.

'But he must be made to talk. Innocent lives are at stake. This thing must be crushed.'

'It wouldn't make any difference if he talked,' Miss Pink said, 'the harm's done now.'

'But I don't understand—'

'Well, you see,' she went on, 'the danger's in the idea, not the person. We'd always thought it couldn't happen here. It could happen in Cyprus or Algeria or South America but we said our national character didn't produce terrorists—and all the time it's been coming nearer—'

'But—the law is there to deal with terrorists!'

'They think they're above the law.'

'That's preposterous. The law can, and will, deal with them. We should have capital punishment.'

'And make martyrs of them? They don't mind whether it's life imprisonment or death or torture—'

'I wasn't proposing—'

'No, but this is world-wide; it's not just in a corner of Wales.'

'Then what do you suggest we do?' In his bewildered old eyes there was a genuine plea for a solution.

'What's wrong?' he begged, 'why do they do it? What do they want?'

'They want to change the system.'

'Change the system? There's nothing wrong with the system; I'm happy with it as it is.'